JOANNA AND THE PIANO

GAVIN THOMSON

MMXVIII

THIS BOOK BELONGS TO

_____

For Scarlett, Sapphire and Satine

1   Joanna Jaws: Take One!

2   Not the nine o'clock news, but nearly!

3   The end of the world is nigh or just a storm in a teacup!

4   What to pack, what not to pack and what can be packed by the packers!

5   As one door closes, another door opens!

6   Camp beds and candles!

7   Wi-Fi Daddy, I need Wi-Fi!

8   Why have one when you can have two!

9   That's grand!

10   Guten tag!

11   Wax on, wax off!

12   Your carriage awaits, Ma'am!

13   Close your eyes and open your ears!

14   Now concentrate, there's a test at the end!

15   The *greenhouse. Or* is it the *treblehouse!*

16   Finally, lesson number nine!

17   Now, what did Herr Mozhoven say!

18   Listen for your number to be called!

19   We'll all get along if we all pull together!

20   What's in a name!

21   A midnight swim with geese!

22   Encore! Encore!

23   On your marks, get set...BAKE!

24   His master's voice!

25   Walk on Ludwig!

26   If music be the food of love, play on!

27   And they call it *puppy love!*

28   It's a hard-knock life!

29   Pride before a fall!

30   Not just a pretty face and a dirty neck!

31   Coming out!

32   Eeny, meeny, miny, moe!

33   Dogs are big scaredy-cats!

34   Dressed to impress!

35   Great balls of chocolate!

36   Back to school!

1
Joanna Jaws: Take One!

"Hi. My name's Joanna, and I'm ten years old, and I'm a girl...uh, uh, that's dumb, start again!" exclaims Joanna. She stops *record* and deletes the video, before ridiculing herself. "Of course, they know I'm a girl - they can see that on the video, stupid! And how many boys do they know called Joanna!"

Joanna practises again in her bedroom mirror until she feels confident she's perfected the bubbly and sassy persona, all *vloggers* possess. She brushes her hair for the ninth time and applies a little more make-up from the dressing-up set she received in last year's Santa sack - red blusher and a little blue lipstick! Funky!

She checks the bedroom door is shut and takes her position in front of her computer again - purposefully placed to include her eclectic mix of wall posters behind and where the light seems to give the best natural ambience which she fervently hopes will replicate other videos that regularly entertain and captivate.

Joanna thinks to herself, how funny it is - usually, when asked to do anything in front of anybody, she's generally overcome with shyness and reluctance. But given this apparent anonymity, even though the audience could reach millions, it feels like a chat with her friends in the school playground.

How positively liberating is that!?

"*Joanna Jaws: Take Two*," she says out loud for final motivation, before pressing *record* again.

Jaws isn't her surname, but she likes the alliteration - the suggestion of *talking* and having something *biting* to say...somehow it sounds so much more memorable and edgy than a video blog by Joanna Pulton!

"Hi. My name's Joanna, and I'm ten years old. I live in the best city in the world - *Landan!*" she begins, adopting a slightly American and chatty undertone, "Welcome to my life - the life of a typical ten-year-old girl who wants to be your friend. As you can see, I have long straight brown hair, although my Mother, whose name is Trish, says its more auburn than brown, whatever auburn is! My eyes are hazelnut brown..." describes Joanna as she leans into the tiny *peephole* camera to give everyone an enlarged close-up, "...although in some lights and depending on what I'm wearing, they can appear green!

My right eye is slightly smaller than my left. I have brown eyebrows and eyelashes, and my cheeks are slightly freckled," continues Joanna as she pulls back again. "My mother says I have inherited my skin colour from my grandmother, Grandma Mo, her mother - she's from Jamaica in The Caribbean - who married my grandfather, Grandpa Jo - an Englishman from North London, who fell in love with her in the days when it's frowned upon for different ethnic groups to marry. Can you believe it!?" exclaims Joanna as she pulls a face to mock this absurdity and shakes her head fiercely to emphasise her disapproval. "Anyway, my mother says I still have to be careful in the sun as everyone must practise *safe sun - skin damage is skin damage, whatever your skin colour*," preaches Joanna as she mimics her mother with a fake adult voice and finger-pointing, before breaking into a huge smile. "Yes, I wear braces - *train tracks* top and bottom.

something to do with a *crossbite*, a slight *underbite* and *teeth crowding!* I love and hate them. I love them because I get to miss some school every six weeks…I get to choose what colour wire holders - now blue and I know I'm going to have beautiful teeth at the end of it all…but I hate them because I can't eat certain things like oranges, nuts or chewy sweets and cleaning is a real nightmare. I don't just have one brush, but several, to work in between and behind the wires and not just twice a day, but after every meal!" relays Joanna, licking her lips and sweeping her tongue across her braces in a similar manner to a nose cleaning cow. "But enough about my braces! It's not like I'm the only person in the world to wear braces and even if I were, it's not that exciting!" admits Joanna as she makes a fake yawn and pats her mouth several times in self-mocking. "What else can I tell you about me? I'm 133 centimetres tall. That's four foot four. Not big and not small. Pretty average. I weigh 31 kilograms. That's five stone 2 pounds. Again, not light and not heavy. Pretty average. I'm left-handed. My shoe size is 4, although my right foot is slightly longer than my left. I take a *G* fitting, which means my feet are quite wide and sometimes I can't have the shoes I want because my parents don't want me to get bunions…like my Grandma Mo. Apparently, it's a real pain!" says Joanna, losing focus for a second and averting her eyes to the side, to reach over and grab her fancy-framed family photo. "This is me with my Mum and Dad," she says, proudly pointing at the recent photo taken by a stranger as they stand outside *Il Duomo* during this summer's Tuscan holiday. "My Dad's called Roger - he's an engineer and my Mum's called Trish as I said earlier - she's a housewife, but used to be in publishing. She keeps trying to write her first novel, but *never gets around to it!*" quotes Joanna, with hand-gestured quote marks, more resembling rabbit shadow puppets than grammatical intonation! "My Dad keeps pulling her leg...something about *pigs flying* and *hell freezing over!* Maybe one day I'll introduce them to you in person, but perhaps not...I wouldn't want to subject anyone to my Dad's terrible jokes or my Mum's nagging - *Joanna, clean your room - Joanna, don't leave your shoes at the bottom of the stairs - Joanna, don't slurp your tea!*" again mimics Joanna, wagging the same finger and putting on the same fake adult voice. "I don't have any brothers or sisters. I think my Mum and Dad wanted another child, but there were complications. We don't talk about it. Anyway, I like being the centre of attention and being spoiled, although sometimes it would be nice to have a little brother to tease and poke fun...*Girl-Power!*" smirks Joanna as she tries to impersonate Mr Universe if the universe were made up of puny ten-year-old girls! "So, that's pretty much an introduction into me. I hope you enjoyed it. Next time on *Joanna Jaws*, I'm going to talk about my likes and dislikes. Should be fun! So, *keep smiling*. 'Till next time. Stinky boy, boy!"

And with that, Joanna taps the *stop* button, saves the video to a desktop file named *Top Secret*, uploads it to her video channel, tweets, snaps and sends out notifications to all her friends. "I wonder how many *likes* I'll get," she whispers to herself. "I hope it's more than Becky Winston!"

2

Not the nine o'clock news, but nearly!

"Jo...anna," calls Joanna's Mum, Trish. "Please, come down. I need to talk to you."

"Yes, please, come down," echoes Joanna's Dad, Roger. "We have something important to talk to you about."

Joanna tuts and rolls her eyes at her friend, Jenny. "Sorry, Jen!" apologises Joanna, "Gotta go. I'll call you back in five. Don't do any more on our scheme 'till I get back."

"No problem," replies Jenny, "I've gotta go, too. My Nan's just arrived."

And with that, both girls tap the *stop* button and watch their images disappear. Their computers become inanimate again - put to sleep as if given a chance to recoup, gather more energy and prepare for the next dramatic interlude...it's hard work keeping up with the imagination and discovery of the modern ten-year-old!

Joanna tears downstairs, sliding her hands down the familiar bannister, now well-worn through constant rubbing and reassurance - through the hall, pulling her fingers along the wall as if she's gliding through long grass in a summer-soiled meadow and into the kitchen. Trish and Roger are sitting at the breakfast bar, sipping coffee and surrounded by streams of papers, strewn haphazardly before them.

"What's up?" asks Joanna as she hoists herself onto the chrome and black stool, barely able to reach the foot rail. Instead, feet dangling like door chimes in a cool autumn breeze.

"Well, you know how Daddy was made redundant recently," begins Trish.

"More of a restructure than redundant," defends Roger, keen to be consistent and appear needed rather than discarded.

"Exactly, Daddy," agrees Trish, "I mean, when Daddy's firm restructured and no longer needed his division..."

Joanna glazes over at this point. Adult semantics and nuances pass her by and fly over her head like low-flying paper planes. All she knows is that her Dad lost his job and he's been at home on *gardening leave* for the last three months, and what a misnomer that is because she hasn't as much seen him mow the lawn, let alone tend to the constant demands of weeds!

She daydreams how *weeds* should be called *strongs* and how some are quite pretty...

"...well, Daddy has some great news," continues Trish as she raises a smile and directs her eyes to Roger, giving him a nod like a play's prompter, supplying the lines to a frozen actor, "...haven't you, Daddy?"

"Yes, Darling," grins Roger as his eyes widen and a smile begins to beam, revealing shining white teeth that sparkle on his face and illuminate his demeanour. "Daddy's got a new job!"

"That's brilliant, Daddy!" praises Joanna as she jumps from her stool and throws her arms around his waist, squeezing as tightly as she can and mimicking his hugs whenever she does anything wonderful or praiseworthy.

"Thank you, Sweetheart," replies Roger, delighted with such a warm response and stroking her hair with his enormous hands that seem to engulf her head like a swimmer's hat, "however, there is something else..."

Joanna relaxes her hold and steps back, staring into her father's eyes with a look of uncertainty. She's old enough to realise that whenever a sentence begins with, *however*, it more than likely results in a negative remark rather than a positive one!

"...my new job is in a different part of the country," continues Roger.

"Yes, dear," adds Trish, "and unfortunately it's not a straightforward commute."

Joanna is confused. She has no perspective of commuting length or distance - anything longer than ten minutes feels like a lifetime. People don't joke about kids moaning *are we there yet?* For no reason!

"Mummy and I have been doing a lot of thinking," adds Roger, "and weighing everything up..."

"...what with you ready to start big school, soon," assists Trish, "and now being as good a time as any..."

"...for us to move to a new house," finally blurts Roger, breathing out heavily, as if a huge weight is lifted from him. "To make a fresh start!"

Joanna is speechless. Like her computer upstairs, her brain is listening, digesting and taking time to compute what this means.

"Living here in the city," adds Trish, "means our house is worth a lot of money which goes a lot further in the countryside..."

"...so, we've found this amazing manor house in the country," enthuses Roger, "with lots of grounds and a lake..."

"...it's a bit run down and needs work," admits Trish, "but it will make a fantastic home, Darling. Somewhere we can all be very happy."

Joanna has been silent long enough.

"I don't want to move," shouts Joanna, annoyed her parents haven't asked her and presented her with a *fait accompli*. "I'm happy here. This is my home. It's where I was born and where I grew up. It's where all my friends are."

"You'll make new friends," replies Roger, thinking this will make sense to a ten-year-old. Instead, it acted like a red rag to a bull.

"I won't!" screams Joanna, now with tears cascading down her cheeks, as if sent by her brain to extinguish the fire in her mouth. "I hate you. I hate you!" further screams Joanna, trying to use her stare to inflict pain on both her parents, before running out of the kitchen as a last act of defiance. "I hate you!"

"But, Darling..." says Roger, saddened.

"Leave her," calms Trish, placing her hand on his arm and pressing, as if trying to stop the bleeding from his wound. "She's angry, but she'll come around."

"We should've spoken about this before..." annoys Roger, "...involved her in the process somehow."

"But everything was in the air," reasons Trish. "We only found out today. It would've been more confusing to juggle with her emotions on a possibility that might never happen."

"But I think we forget she's growing up," realises Roger. "She's not a little girl anymore. She's bright and confronting her own issues, and on the brink of becoming a young woman."

"But she's just a child, Roger," replies Trish, "and sometimes children just need to be children and not have to carry the burdens of adult life or emotions they're not equipped to rationalise or reason."

"She's an only child, Trish," replies Roger. "She can't help but be more mature and part of our world. I think we've underestimated her."

"She'll be fine, Roger," reassures Trish. "Her strength *is* being an only child. Her ability to know herself and be happy on her own - not as a loner, but happy spending time on her own...in her own world."

"I just want her to be happy," nods Roger, looking to Trish for a similar response.

"She will be...she is," replies Trish, reaching over to kiss Roger on the cheek and add a mother's intuition. "If we're happy, then she'll be happy. It's just part and parcel of making big, life-changing decisions...and being parents!"

"I hope so," sighs Roger, sipping the last of his coffee - now aptly cold, as he collects and collates the strewn papers into one neat pile. "I do hope so."

3

The end of the world is nigh
or just a storm in a teacup!

"C'mon Jenny, pick up!" annoys Joanna as she wipes her last few tears on *Snonkey*, "Why do five minutes never mean five minutes!"

Snonkey is Joanna's faithful and much-loved, stuffed snow-white donkey, has been with her since her second birthday and fell in love with him, the minute she laid eyes on him. She can't remember for sure but thinks he was a present from her Aunty Vie - short for Viola, her Mum's sister.

Those were the days when Joanna's other best friends were her left and right thumbs! Most children favour the left or right, but Joanna wasn't fussy - whichever *smelled* or *tasted* the best, went straight into her mouth like a cork being wedged into a vintage wine, only to be *uncorked* at meal or snack times, when the substitute seemed a fair swap!

To call Snonkey *snow-white* is a far stretch. After eight years of hard-hugging, head-resting, floor-dragging, machine-washing, sun-drying, mouth-sucking and wool-twizzling, he's more of a mid-tone grey - the sort of grey not too dissimilar to a freezing February winter's day! Snonkey's red scarf, however - made from silk, has survived the test of time and remains distinctively red, albeit frayed and shortened in length.

Snonkey may be a bit loose at the seams, but in true *Bagpussian spirit*, Joanna loved him!

Joanna waits patiently, outstretched on her bed, front down and lower legs swaying in the air like boughs in the wind - perhaps more like that of a desperate-for-the-loo, leg shaker!

The familiar computer *tring* breaks the silence. It's Jenny. Finally!

"You're not going to believe what's just happened, Jenny," begins Joanna without any attempt at *hello* or, *how are you?* "My world has been turned upside down...worse than that, my world has ended!"

"Slow down, Joanna," replies Jenny, finishing a mouthful of crisps before hard-straw-sipping, as only ten-year-olds hard-straw-sip, the last few drops of her juice carton. "What do you mean your world has ended?"

"We're moving, Jenny!" simply states Joanna, "Leaving the city for the country. *A fresh start* my Dad calls it. *The time's right* my Mum says. Not a single question or concern for what I might have to say about it. I hate them, Jenny. How can they do this to me? They must really hate me."

Jenny suddenly realises the impact on her too - her best friend is leaving her, deserting her. It isn't right. How can Joanna's parents do this to them? Tears begin to fall, fuelled by an enormous well of emotion. They have been friends since the first day of reception class when she consoled Joanna after Teddy Fordman bit her arm and pushed her over in the sandpit!

"You can't go, Joanna," selfishly responds Jenny, trying hard not to show emotion. "I won't let it happen. There must be something we can do - some way we can get your parents to change their mind."

"They won't change their minds," concedes Joanna. "My Dad just got a new job, and we have to move to be close to it."

"Perhaps we can run away," suggests Jenny, "or hide in my shed at the bottom of my garden. No one will ever find us there, and we can get my brother to bring us food in secret!"

Honk-honk sounds Joanna's computer. It's the sound she programmed to denote a new email. A little box appears in the bottom right corner, highlighting *one new message: Message from Daddy: with attachment.*

"Hang on a sec, Jenny," replies Joanna as she finger-scrolls the miniature mousepad with one hand and finger-clicks to open the email with the other. "I've got an email from my Dad. I'll send it to you so we can both look at it at the same time...one sec...there. It's gone."

"Got it," eagerly responds Jenny, "I'm opening it now."

Both their screens divide into segments - the left majority, displays the email while the top right, presents a respective rectangular view of each other, both containing yet another smaller rectangle showing the view as seen by the other! There isn't a hint of amazement or questioning of how this is achieved, but an expectation of this as the norm - two ten-year-olds communicating from their bedrooms like this is how it's always been!

Joanna reads the message aloud. "*Dearest Joanna, I'm sorry if this is a shock to you. It wasn't our intention to upset you or exclude you. It just happened so fast, and we did what we thought best for us all. Perhaps the attached will get you excited and don't ever think you're leaving everything behind. Your friends will always be* always welcome, and we will, of course, be coming back to catch up with friends. How can we not, when your Aunty Vie still lives here. Love Daddy. X times a million."

"Shall we open the attachment?" asks Jenny, not wanting to presume or further upset Joanna.

"Let's go for it," advises Joanna, "...it's probably one of his stupid jokes he finds on the internet!"

It isn't. It's an estate agency brochure, describing and portraying Joanna's new home!

"O.M.G!" shrills Jenny, "This is a palace!"

Joanna is speechless. She repeatedly clicks the right arrow of the onscreen brochure, flabbergasted by each unfurling image. Yes *it's a little run down* as her Mum says and yes, *it needs work,* but it's annoyingly amazing!

As Joanna comes to the end of the picture show, she clicks back to the beginning and reads the summary description aloud "Originally an Elizabethan manor house, owned by Sir Francis Drake's sister and brother-in-law, Fortuna House was significantly extended in the eighteenth-century by Henry and Liza Bucket, the family who made their fortune patenting a metal construction 'bucket', the name of which carries through to this day and whose revolutionary design was responsible for changing the face of modern agriculture and building construction. Grade II listed and boasting many of these original and unchanged features, Fortuna House has four large reception rooms, two further studies, large kitchen with scullery, utility and wine cellar, hallway leading to an impressive double stairway to the first floor. Four en-suite double bedrooms and rear staircase leading to top floor. Four further bedrooms are sharing two family-sized bathrooms. *Storage rooms. Land includes two acres of formal gardens and paddock. Stables. Lake with a boathouse. Orangery. Long sweeping drive. Although in need of modernisation, Fortuna House must be viewed. Its charm comes in buckets!"*

"Your world definitely hasn't ended, Joanna!" remarks Jenny, tinged with a mixture of excitement and envy. "This is your very own castle...and you're the princess!"

"But I don't want to move!" replies Joanna, still upset with her parents.

"Your parents can't hate you, Joanna!" says Jenny, trying to convince Joanna, "This is *beyond* beyond!"

"I feel terrible," worries Joanna. "I repeatedly told my parents how I hated them, especially my Dad. How will they forgive me?"

"Of course, they'll forgive you, Joanna," consoles Jenny, "...they love you and know you don't mean it. My Mum would say *it's just another storm in a teacup in the life of a ten-year-old!"*

"Thanks, Jenny, you're a great friend," finishes Joanna, feeling sheepish and embarrassed at her earlier outburst. "I better go and apologise. See you tomorrow?"

"You betcha!" replies Jenny. "Just try and stop me."

4

What to pack, what not to pack
and what can be packed by the packers!

"Joanna, please go and start packing," asks Trish as she enters the living room, clutching or rather struggling with a large brown cardboard box, labelled *Trish's Toiletries!* "We're moving tomorrow, and we have to be out by nine before the moving company arrives."

"Yes, yes, Mummy," replies Joanna, not listening. She thinks this will buy her more time to watch the latest *must-see, can't be missed, best show e-ver!* "I'm on it."

"Seriously, Joanna. I mean now. Turn that rubbish off and start packing!" snaps Trish, losing patience and realising her underestimation for how long it takes to box, tape and label a decade of family life. "You only have your room to do. That's all."

Joanna tuts and rolls her eyes. This is her typical response when asked to do anything she doesn't want to do! Her Dad jokes about it being a disease and how he knew one girl that kept rolling her eyes so often that one day they rolled all the way back in her head and never rolled back again and that's where the expression *inward-looking* comes!

Joanna knows she can't put off packing any longer, so turns off the TV and makes her way upstairs. She passes her Dad on the landing - he's wearing his *DIY clothes!* Other Dads she knows, have a pair of fancy overalls, ordinarily blue, or look perfectly primed with cool jeans, rugged lumberjack shirt and a tool-filled, brown suede tool-belt, but not her Dad! Roger wears clothes that have *seen better days* and should have made their way to the bin

- old smart shirts, torn under the arms, now paint speckled and fingerprinted...ancient jeans with inevitable rips in the bottom area and smelly trainers with loose flapping soles that make a funny slapping noise as he walks!

"Lovin' the look, Daddy!" jokes Joanna, "Very gangsta' grime!"

"I didn't realise I lived with the DIY fashion police!" retorts Roger.

"You don't!" replies Joanna, "Otherwise I'd arrest you, put you in jail and throw away the key!"

"You know how to hit a man where it hurts," jokes Roger, holding his right hand to his *shot* heart and fake-staggering backwards. "I've put three boxes in your room. Please, get on with it - it takes longer than you think."

Joanna closes her door and spends the first five minutes choosing the right *packing music* and deciding on speakers or headphones. "Speakers - no risk of entanglement!"

"Right, what first?" poses Joanna as she surveys her room like an owl - feet rooted to the ground, but head revolving almost full circle. "The bookcase!"

Book after book, is stacked carefully into the first box - some hard and square, some soft and rectangular, but most novel-sized and a mixture of both hard and soft covered. Joanna is a keen reader. "This is tiring!" slows Joanna as she sighs a deep sigh, "And so boring!"

Barely ten minutes have passed when soft-limbed *scooping* and random *chucking* replace her initial enthusiasm and order! "I think I deserve a rest. Ooh, I like this song!" and with that, Joanna sits cross-legged on the floor and loses herself in pop music.

The door opens. Trish stands there, simmering like a kettle about to boil. "Is this all you've done in an hour?" she remarks, "C'mon. I don't want to be packing all night!"

"I'm tired," complains Joanna, looking at her mother with *please help me* eyes. "It's too difficult!"

"Alright, Darling," replies Trish, remembering there are certain things ten-year-olds don't do very well - cleaning up after themselves? Certainly not, looking for things and now it would seem - packing! "Let's do it together. You know what they say, Joanna - more hands make less work!"

Joanna loves doing things with her Mum or Dad. Everything seems so much easier, and somehow her opinions suddenly seem to matter.

"What are we doing with these?" asks Trish, wading through a pile of school artworks, "Keep or chuck?"

Joanna sits, sporting a pink dress-up wig and acting as *judge and jury* on each picture her Mum holds up. She uses their acid test - *Picasso or Pollock?* If she can't imagine either artist painting it - *chuck*, if she can - *keep!* Some calls are close and require Trish's second opinion, but it's amazing how many end up in the bin!

They sort Joanna's clothes into winter and summer and put any unwanted items in a box, clearly marked *Charity*. Trish boxed Joanna's baby and toddler clothes many years before, so this exercise turns out to be remarkably quick and thankfully easy!

As much as they try to cull Joanna's vast collection of cuddly toys, both realise this is a decision best made a few more years down the line. Not because Snonkey needs his friends, but each one represents something special!

Trish comes across *her* special cuddly toy - the one she had as a child, the one she nicknamed *Nappy*. "Goodness me, Joanna!" exclaims Trish as she gathers Nappy in her arms and sits at the end of Joanna's bed to rest for a moment, "This takes me back. I remember when I first got her," she begins, beckoning Joanna to sit next to her, which she does, grabbing Snonkey. "Her name was Molly, and she wore this ridiculous outfit, which I despised. One day, I took it off and threw it in the bin - without Grandma or Grandpa knowing...and put a nappy on her! I remember it being a super hot summer and all I seemed to wear was just a nappy..."

"...was this at school?" leg-pulls Joanna.

"Nooo, silly, I was only two, going on three!" replies Trish, suddenly realising, Joanna is making a joke, "But I also called her Nappy because she has eyes that close when you lay her down...see...and I wouldn't go to sleep or take a *nappy* without my Nappy! Seems so stupid now."

"I don't think so, Mummy," says Joanna, "she's part of you."

"Like you are part of me," replies Trish, hugging Joanna and placing her chin on Joanna's head.

"Like Snonkey's part of me," adds Joanna, hugging Snonkey, "and this house."

"And now our new house," adds Trish, "or rather our new home, the new home we can build together - as a family...the new home where we can create lifelong memories, together."

"As a family," replies Joanna as she squeezes tighter, "...create lifelong memories, together...as a family."

"Exactly, Joanna!" reassures Trish - some of which she aims at Joanna and the rest she aims at herself, "New starts are scary and daunting for everyone - even your Daddy and I are scared!"

24

5

As one door closes, another door opens!

"Please, put your seatbelt on, Joanna," instructs Roger as he turns the key in the ignition. "Remember, it's the law!"

"Do I have to?" moans Joanna, as she grapples with her bed pillow, "I want to lie down and fall asleep."

"You have to fasten your seatbelt, Darling," reaffirms Trish. "We don't want you flying through the windscreen if we have an accident. Why don't you prop your pillow against the door and snuggle into it that way? I'm sure you'll fall asleep as soon as we start moving. It looks like Snonkey's already dozed off!"

"It's so annoying!" complains Joanna, as she does as she's told and prepares herself for upright sleeping. "How long is it again?"

"It's a six-hour drive!" replies Roger, "But we'll stop every two hours for a break. Let me put the back-of-seat television on for you. That should help pass the time when you're not sleeping."

"Thanks, Daddy!" yawns Joanna, "You're the best!"

Roger puts on his seatbelt and checks his mirrors. He can barely see out of the rear window with all the boxed essentials, including, of course, *Regina*, Joanna's female *Rex* rabbit.

"Quick *check* please, Trish," asks Roger.

"Good idea, Roger," replies Trish, as she looks at her list. "New address to the movers?"

"Check," nods Roger with a wry smile. "Wouldn't that be a disaster!"

"Estate agents primed with keys and cleaning instructions?" reads Trish.

"Check," nods Roger.

"Gas and electric meter readings?" reads Trish.

"Check, check," nods Roger, again with a wry smile, impressed at their excellent teamwork.

"Post diverted?" reads Trish.

"Check," nods Roger.

"Keys to our new home?" reads Trish.

"We pick them up from the agents when we arrive," confirms Roger.

"Then we're good to go!" informs Trish, "This is it. Goodbye old home. We won't forget you!"

"Yes, goodbye old home!" adds Roger, "Thank you for all the good times!"

"Bye-bye, old home!" pipes up Joanna, "I'm gonna miss you."

Joanna put on a brave face - still sad and annoyed to be leaving, upset at saying goodbye to *lifelong* friends, nervous and apprehensive of what lies ahead. Butterflies ferociously flutter in her tummy whenever she thinks about it!

"Anyone need a pee?" enquires Roger, noting a shake of heads, "And did everyone remember to pack a sense of humour?" he quips, this time noting a nod of heads, "Right. We're off!"

And with that, Roger indicates right and drives out of the gate for the last time - their old house fading into the distance like end credits of a film. It's not long before they hit the motorway and join the monotony of high-speed driving. Old house? What old house!?

"Can we play the *car game?*" asks Joanna as she awakes from forty winks - stretching her arms and shaking her head like a snow globe being whisked into life.

"I'll be blue," selects Roger.

"I'll be red," chooses Trish.

"Ohh, I wanted to be red," complains Joanna.

"OK, you be red," surrenders Trish, "and I'll be white."

"You can't be white or black or silver," instructs Roger, "it's an unfair advantage."

"Sorry, Sir!" jests Trish with a salute, "Then I'll be yellow."

"One!" shouts Roger as he spies a blue car in his rear-view mirror.

"It doesn't count, Daddy!" protests Joanna, "It has to be cars on the other side - cars coming towards us."

"I can't believe how such a simple game can be so complicated!" observes Trish, shaking her head in disbelief before her competitive side takes over. "One...two...three!"

"No, Mummy!" again protests Joanna, "We haven't said *start!*"

"Oh, very well," concedes Trish. "Start...one...two...three!"

The game is played with intensity for about half an hour before a cloud of lethargy descends - Joanna snuggles into her pillow and falls asleep again, aided by the hypnotical repetition of white stripes and cat's eyes. Trish checks her emails and sends a response text to her sister, telling her where to find the box of groceries they left for her. Roger stays focused, occasionally indicating to overtake, overtaking, then shifting back in the middle lane.

"Pit stop!" declares Roger as he sees the one-mile sign for services, "Petrol, pee and a pot of tea!"

"I'm dying for a coffee," declares Trish, "I've normally had four by now!"

"Joanna, wake up, darling," murmurs Roger, "we're at the first stop."

Having visited the service station toilets, which is always an experience - joining the *steady stream* of strangers and sharing the most basic of human bodily functions, they sit at a café table next to the window. They choose the window because it appears to offer an interesting view. Instead, it presents them with a vehicular regiment of all shapes and sizes, and all makes and models - a cross-section of modern-day motoring, squeezed into an acre of tarmac!

"I can't drink anymore," states Joanna as she pushed away her hot chocolate, having sucked all the cream off the top and demolished all the accompanying marshmallows.

"You've barely touched it!" scolds Roger, "I knew this would happen. It happens every time!"

"Eyes bigger than her stomach," adds Trish, sipping her white americano and relishing every moment. "I told you, Roger. She should've shared your tea."

"Do you want to swap?" Roger asks Joanna, "Your hot chocolate for my second cup of tea?"

"Thanks, Daddy," replies Joanna, turning Roger's tea into a cup of milk with a hint of tea and thrusting a straw into it. "Hot chocolate's too sweet for me!"

The middle section of the journey passes pretty much as the first. Instead of the *car game*, they play three rounds of the *alphabet game*, each in turn, naming animals, then first names, then countries, complaining when someone takes too long and debating whether *Snonkey* is an acceptable first name. A further forty winks for Trish and Joanna, while Roger listens to his preferred radio channel of *indie rock…déjà vu* experiences at the next service station, seemingly with the same layout, the same shops, the same cafes and even the same visitors!

'We're into the final stretch," announces Roger, leaving the motorway - the backdrop changing dramatically and cars diminishing like competitors failing to finish the race. "We'll be there in half an hour. Let's have a sing-song to pass the time."

After the worst rendition of *Sweet Caroline*, an attempt at a Justin Bieber song and three choruses of *Ging Gang Goolie*, they arrive at the estate agents. Roger returns, smile beaming with a noticeable spring in his step and dangling the keys in front of his face like a pendulum clock. Joanna can sense the underlying excitement and anticipation. Although Roger and Trish have seen the house before, it wasn't theirs. It is now!

Five minutes later, they turn into the impressive, *Fortuna House* with its plaque and pillared gateway. They drive slowly, creeping up the drive as if trying not to wake this *sleeping beauty*. Roger stops halfway. There is silence. No one saying anything, just staring - staring at their new home, each imagining themselves inside and the times they're going to have. Roger turns to Trish and then around to Joanna. Serious contemplation turns into smiles. Smiles then turn into grins until they all break into the biggest fit of giggles!

"C'mon girls!" laughs Roger, "Let's go and see our new home."

6

Camp beds and candles!

"The key won't turn," complains Roger, as he slips it into the large white painted door. "I hope the agents gave me the right one!"

"Here, let me try," offers Trish as she takes the key, examines the *Fortuna House* label and tries again. "There you go!" she cries, after a little teasing.

"How did you do that?" asks Roger, looking both puzzled and beaten.

"A woman's knack!" boasts Trish, rubbing her lapel with inturned nails and smiling, "Some of us have got it, and some of us haven't!"

The door swings open and they take their first steps across the threshold. There's a definite musty smell - the smell of a place sitting unoccupied for too long. Joanna learns later that the previous owner - a lady in her nineties, passed away some twelve months previously and she hadn't done any maintenance or renovations since her husband passed away, some thirty years before that. The lady's children, who didn't want to keep the house because it had too many memories, removed most of her possessions, but some sporadically remain like sheet covered ghosts.

"Let's open some windows," suggests Trish, keen to inject some fresh air. "That's better," she declares, opening two sash windows either side of the front door. "Can't beat a bit of country air!"

"So much for our checklist, Trish!" complains Roger, flicking the hall switch up and down several times, as if each time, the lights will magically turn on. "We forgot to get the electricity turned on!"

"I suppose that means the gas, too?" realises Trish, "...and the telephone?"

"I'm not worried about the telephone," replies Roger, speed dialling the estate agents from his mobile. "Yes, hi! Mr Pulton here. Just picked up the keys for Fortuna House...Yes, everything's fine, thank you, except all the utilities are still disconnected. They were supposed to be put on today, but there was a problem, you say..." repeats Roger, aloud, so that Trish can keep up, "...definitely tomorrow morning, you say...Yes, we should be able to manage this evening...it all adds to the excitement as we're planning to camp tonight! Yes, yes...the movers arrive first thing tomorrow with all our belongings. Thank you for your help. Bye."

Roger and Trish shake heads at each other but remain upbeat for Joanna's sake. "Let's not let it spoil the moment," rallies Roger, opening the living room door. "Something had to drop - things were going too well!"

"Wow!" exclaims Joanna, moving from room to room, running upstairs on one staircase and downstairs on the other and then revisiting everywhere to make sure she hasn't missed anything, "Wow, wow, wow!"

"The kitchen needs a good clean, but it's got everything here until we replace it," reasons Trish. "Let me put the kettle on," she offers, grabbing the kettle from the *essentials box*, brought in from the car."

"It won't suit you!" jests Roger.

"Oh, Daddy," sighs Joanna, "not that old joke!"

"Yes, Roger," adds Trish with a slow shake of the head, "perhaps it's time to leave the old jokes in the old house and work on some new ones!" she further adds, blowing him a kiss. "Now I'm being stupid - I forgot there's no electricity!"

"And the wood-burning stove has been converted to gas!" adds Roger, opening the stove fuel door, "I'll get the camping stove."

"Why don't you get the camp beds set up while you're at it and sort out Regina," suggests Trish. "I'll nip to the shops, grab some candles and bring us back a pizza."

"I'll come with you," offers Joanna, "and help you choose the pizza!"

When Trish and Joanna arrive back, Roger has erected three beds in the drawing room, all window-facing and positioned to see the sunset sparkling on the lake. He also found some candles in one of the cupboards.

"This is beautiful, Roger..." commends Trish, "...verging on romantic!"

"I love candles," declares Joanna. "They give a special flickering light that makes the room move and seem alive!"

"That's a clever way of describing it, Joanna," compliments Roger as he rubs his stomach. "Now, what pizza did you get?"

"We got a large one with *half and half*," informs Joanna, "half *pepperoni* for Mummy and me and half *meat feast* with extra mushrooms for you!"

"So not *mush-room* for any other toppings!" quips Roger, now realising his awful puns must stop.

"I'm ignoring that, Daddy!" replies Joanna, "Because you're such a fun guy! Get it? Fungi, fun-guy! ...I'll get our coats!"

The three of them perch on their camp beds and chomp through the pizza before getting ready for bed and nestling into their sleeping bags. Roger positions his torch close to hand after extinguishing the candles and akin to *The Waltons*, they lie, looking out across the lake and chat.

"What a long day," starts Roger, "I'm beat!"

"Tomorrow's going to be just as long, if not longer!" points out Trish.

"But then we'll have our stuff," adds Joanna, "and our comfy beds!"

"I like your thinking!" agrees Trish, "...not sure how much sleep I'm going to get on this bed!"

"This reminds me of the time your Grandad took your Grandma, your Uncle and I camping, Joanna," reminisces Roger. "He bought this four-person tent, two put-you-up beds and two mats. Now, this all sounds fine, but being the novices, we were, we pitched the tent on a slight gradient. Grandma and Grandad, who of course had the put-you-ups, were fine as they lay with their heads *up* the slope. Your Uncle Sean and I, however, had the mats and were told to sleep with our heads furthest away...something about snoring and keeping Grandma awake...which happens to be completely wrong - it's Grandma who can snore for England, as it turns out! Anyway, the next morning, we awake very early, after an awful night's sleep. All the blood has rushed to our heads, and words can't describe the pain, Sean and I were feeling. *Pins and needles* felt more like *nails and screws!* It was a good thirty minutes before we regained the feeling in our feet! Needless to say - we never went camping again!"

"I hate pins and needles!" replies Joanna, "...that and hiccups!"

"That story reminds me of a time I went on holiday with an old boyfriend," begins Trish.

"Not Daddy?" asks Joanna, suddenly super-interested and intrigued.

"No, not Daddy!" replies Trish, "A guy called Luke."

"Here we go!" adds Roger, sounding slightly jealous, *"Cool Hand Luke!"*

"Anyway," ignores Trish, "we ended up camping for one night in a French campsite. That, in itself, is no story, but we turned up with the tiniest of tents and a small gas stove, but nothing else. We paid the fees and found our site, only to be surrounded by families with large caravans, outdoor fridges, huge TVs with satellite dishes, dining tables and chairs and even some with table tennis! Our tent looked pathetic, pitched in this huge area, rather like an old city cottage, defiantly standing as skyscrapers are built around. Anyway, I managed to sweet talk a saucepan from someone, and we cooked pasta, straining it in a fork-pierced plastic bag while those about us tucked into BBQ steak and oven-baked accompaniments. It was hilarious!"

"What happened to Luke?" enquires Joanna, with a hint of mischief.

"Oh, we drifted apart," replies Trish, "and then I met your Daddy!"

"So, what do we think about our new home?" poses Roger, looking to change the subject.

"It's brilliant, Daddy!" replies Joanna, "I can't wait to explore further and get my room sorted."

"I think we're going to be very happy here," adds Trish, "once we get the utilities switched on!"

"I think so, too," agrees Roger, rolling onto his side. "Night-night."

"Yes, night all," replies Trish, sounding a huge yawn.

"Night, Daddy, night, Mummy," adds Joanna, "see you in the morning."

7

Wi-Fi Daddy, I need Wi-Fi!

"Wakey, wakey, Joanna," Roger whispers loudly. "Look outside on the lawn!"

"Ahh! Bunny rabbits!" admires Joanna fondly, rubbing sleep and focusing her eyes like a zooming *in and out* camera lens. "Regina's gonna be in rabbit heaven!"

"I wish that were true," informs Roger, again whispering, so as not to wake Trish, "but sometimes, wild rabbits carry diseases that kill pet rabbits, so we have to be extra careful. Either way, it's lovely watching them bobbing up from their warren and hopping around in the early morning dew. Shall we go and make a cup of tea to surprise Mummy?"

"I'm awake!" exclaims Trish with eyes shut. "I've been awake since four o'clock!"

The three of them stand at the windows, tea in hand and pyjama-clad - counting rabbits. It's seven-fifteen. The sun is trying to shine through the trees and rhododendrons but will have to wait a few more hours to jump over and be seen properly.

There's a knock at the door!

"We're a little early, Mr Pulton," apologises the green overalled man, standing at the door, "but we thought it might suit you for us to make an early start…"

"Goodness!" exclaims Roger, standing in his pyjamas and feeling self-conscious, "Absolutely! Excuse me for not being dressed, but we weren't expecting you for another hour."

"Really sorry about that...but that's terrific!" replies the green overalled man, turning around to give his three bacon-butty-eating colleagues the thumbs up. "The sooner we get started, the sooner we'll be out of your hair!"

Roger quickly dresses, while Trish and Joanna prepare four strong teas - three with two sugars and one with three!

The green overalled man agrees on names for each room, writing big black marker, using brown cardboard corresponding labels and sticking them outside each room with teeth-torn packing tape. "It makes life a lot easier, Mr Pulton," lectures the green overalled man, whom Roger now refers to as *John*.

"I like it, John," replies Roger, also a stickler for systems and efficiency. "Easier for us all!"

Tea-fuelled, the movers begin bringing boxes and depositing them with military-like precision - sometimes two supporting each end and shuffling, crablike, sometimes three, with one man offering extra middle support, but mostly individually, resembling a line of ants, carrying fragmented leaves along the jungle floor...over logs, around trees and back to the nest. Trish and Joanna can't make tea quickly enough, while Roger makes jokes about hollow legs, which the movers have obviously heard many times, judging by their less than enthusiastic responses!

There's another knock at the door - already open, Roger turns to see an orange overalled man standing with a toolbox in hand. "Electricity board, Sir," the man announces with slight hesitation, given the day-late service.

"Fantastic!" replies Roger as a blue overalled man hovers behind the orange overalled man. "You must be from the Gas board?"

"That's right, Sir," replies the blue overalled man, "and I've just seen the telephone company pull up."

"You're like buses!" jokes Roger as he spies a red overalled woman, making her way to the front door, also with a toolbox in hand. "You wait for one, and then three come along at the same time!"

Roger gives Trish the thumbs up and signals another three teas. It's not long before the house is a hive of activity - a colour-coded scene of crisscrossing and near misses! Then nothing. It's lunchtime.

Green overalls congregate outside, laughing and swapping stories, as they unclick sturdy lunch boxes and devour the contents in seconds. *Red, blue and orange overalls* stay by their work, calmly sitting on closed toolboxes, pouring cups of flask coffee and slowly nibbling home-made sandwiches - *red* has made tuna with cucumber on a brown roll, *blue* has made ham with cheese and pickle on thick white bread, *orange* has made egg with tomato on brown seeded bread.

Meanwhile, Roger, Trish and Joanna have takeaway pizza...again. Not last night's leftovers, but Trish picked up more when she popped out for extra milk, sugar and...tea!

"We can see the light at the end of the tunnel!" says John as he passes Roger, Trish and Joanna, sitting outside on kitchen chairs - pizza boxes scattered at their feet. "Just the beds, fridge and freezer, sofas and tables and we're done. About an hour and a half, I'd say."

"Wonderful!" exclaims Trish, cuddling Joanna.

"Cool bananas!" adds Joanna, giving John the thumbs up and making him giggle at the thought of bananas being *cool!*

There's a noticeable change in pace after lunch - before lunch, there was a sense of urgency, after lunch, it's as if someone's pressed the *slow-motion* button! Everybody's blood is more interested in digesting food, as limbs move like slowly cranking steam-driven machinery, overcoming gravity and inertia.

Joanna gets excited as two green overalls mountaineer her bed upstairs and into her bedroom. She turns to Roger. "Can I go and unpack and start settling in?" she asks, grasping two hands together, prayer-like. "Pleeease, Daddy!"

"Very well, Darling," replies Roger, recognising Joanna's contribution, although highly appreciated, is waning. "That sounds like a good idea."

As Joanna races upstairs, she sees the orange and blue overall-wearing men shake Roger's hand, issue him with a list of completed works and leave, before hearing him shout, "Hey, Trish, we have lift off!" as he bounds into the kitchen, turning on lights, rubbing his hands and saying, "let's kick this stove into life!"

Joanna begins moving a few things around and unpacking a box of desk items, but just as packing had been tiring and boring, so, it now appears, is unpacking! It's not long before Joanna loses interest and looks for something else to do. "I know," she thinks to herself, grabbing her computer from the box, plugging it in and mentally commenting on the antique sockets, "I'll call Jenny."

The computer *trings*, trying to make contact before displaying *call failed*. Joanna tries again, but with the same result. "There's no

Wi-Fi!" she exclaims, "Surely the red overalled woman has finished by now?"

Joanna runs downstairs, taking care not to trip or disturb the green-overall men as they finish moving in the last few items. She sees her Dad talking with the red overalled woman - the woman who stands between her and Jenny! "When will the Wi-Fi be ready, Daddy?" asks Joanna, appearing slightly rude as she interrupts the conversation.

"It appears we may have to wait up to ten days!" relays Roger with frustration in his voice.

"I'm sorry, Pet!" apologises the red overalled woman, whom Joanna can see by a lapel badge, is called Beth. "I was explaining to your Dad. There has never been Wi-Fi here, and the telephone cable needs to be replaced with an up-to-date, high speed, fibre-optic cable."

"No Wi-Fi!" cries Joanna, "Ten days you say?" she further cries, "But I need Wi-Fi! I need Wi-Fi to talk to my friends!"

"I'm really sorry, Pet!" apologises Beth again, "I wish I could do something, but I can't!"

8

Why have one when you can have two!

"Pass the cornflakes please, Joanna," asks Trish as she sits down, having grabbed a spoon and bowl from the cupboard, "I fancy a bowl this morning."

"I'm hurt!" jests Roger from behind his newspaper - Trish and Joanna looking at each other with confused gazes...before he lowers his newspaper and adds, "You fancy a bowl and not me!"

Audible sighs fill the room, and Roger raises his newspaper to hide behind completely. "I'm wasted here!" he blurts, "Let's see if there are any jobs advertised for unappreciated comedians!"

It's been a week since they arrived - still no Wi-Fi and cardboard boxes still litter the house like chess pieces, diminishing daily like chess pawns taken by an opposing knight or bishop. Roger has four more weeks before he starts his new job and Joanna has four more weeks before she starts her new school. Every day is task-filled from dusk 'til dawn.

"Have you thought any more about what you want to do in your room, Joanna?" quizzes Trish as she chews noisily another spoon of cornflakes. "Perhaps we can make a start on it today, while Daddy finishes tiling our en-suite bathroom."

"I'm going to get Jim to do that," responds Roger, folding the newspaper and grabbing his mug of tea. "Perhaps I can help Joanna, while you finish the curtains for the living room."

Jim is a hired hand - a local tradesman...a *jack-of-all-trades*, Roger describes him. Someone they have employed for six months to help restore and renovate this otherwise, overly daunting project. Jim lives in an old hunting lodge within the grounds of Fortuna House - he starts at nine and finishes at five, six days a week.

"Sounds like a good plan," replies Trish, scooping the last mouthful of milk, before pushing away her bowl and spoon. "Happy with that, Joanna?"

"Sure," replies Joanna, munching on marmite and peanut butter toast and eating everything except the crusts, "I know what I want my theme to be. I've planned it here," adds Joanna, opening her notebook, labelled *Joanna Jaws* and turning to the double-page spread, entitled *My Room!* "I'm thinking everything pure white, pink feature wall, bronze accessories and black highlights!"

Roger and Trish look at each other as if they've discovered the next interior design superstar, both slightly agog!

Usually, Joanna would use her computer and make a *PowerPoint* presentation, but since there's no Wi-Fi, she's had to resort to good old-fashioned hand-creations. This method has grown on her because she gets to feel tangible things rather than just look.

"This is my inspiration," continues Joanna, unfolding a magazine cutout, "and this is the pink swatch..." she adds, showing a pencil-crossed *princess pink* from one of the paint swatch books, Trish picked up the day before, "...and these are some of the things I'd like," she further adds, showing a collage of different magazine cutouts, "...this bronze wall clock, this bronze bedside table lamp and this wall mirror, which we could spray with bronze spray paint. Some blackboards, which we could make ourselves, a black

"I like a girl who knows her own mind," applauds Trish. "Like mother like daughter!"

"I think it's very tasteful, Darling," compliments Roger, "and pretty easy to achieve. We'll nip to the paint shop straight after breakfast and then make a start."

Joanna's smile beams from ear to ear - she's slightly stunned by the positive response!

"Your decision to paint the wall opposite the window, pink, is definitely the right one, Joanna," remarks Roger, taking three steps back to admire his handiwork, "and this tone of pink..."

"...princess pink!" corrects Joanna.

"...and this tone of *princess pink!*" repeats Roger, smiling fondly at Joanna, "...really suits this size of room and isn't too garish."

"Do you think Mummy can make me some white curtains, trimmed with white lace?" asks Joanna, standing in front of the window and making sweeping, windmill-like arm gestures.

"I'm sure she can," replies Roger. "She's a whizz with a sewing machine! I, on the other hand, end up sewing like a slithering snake, waving seams and sometimes double-sewing bits together by mistake!"

"It's a shame we have to ruin the effect of this room by putting in my bookshelf and all my school stuff," remarks Joanna, "I don't think princesses live like that!"

"Now that's a thought," says Roger, pressing the lid back on the pink paint pot and wrapping his paintbrush in cellophane, ready for the second coat, "we don't have to put them in here."

"What do you mean, Daddy?" enquires Joanna, intrigued by his comment.

"Why don't you have a second room?" suggests Roger, pointing his finger upwards like an overly enthusiastic schoolboy, bursting to tell the answer, "We've got another floor, full of rooms. I'm having a study up there. Your mother wants a serene *writing* room. So why don't you have a workroom up there?"

"My own playroom," excites Joanna, beginning to imagine it. "My very own video-recording room!"

"Exactly," agrees Roger, "your very own playroom, where you can study and entertain friends. Let's go upstairs and choose a room for you. I haven't looked properly upstairs, so we can kill two birds with one stone."

Roger is still wearing his old DIY clothes and *flapping-sole-slaps* his way upstairs, closely followed by Joanna.

"I think your Mother said she wanted the back-left room," remembers Roger, opening its door. "Yes, she said there was a pretty fireplace with blue-flowered tiles, and there it is, there!"

Roger opens another door to find a bathroom, then another to find a storage room with no window, then another to find another bathroom, and then another - almost an exact mirror image of Trish's favoured room. "I think I'll have this room," he decides, nodding his head and completing a quick lap. "The light's perfect and I love the view of the lake."

"So that leaves one of the two front rooms," says Joanna, hoping she hasn't been dealt the short straw. They do a quick tour of both rooms. Like the back two bedrooms, they are mirror images of each other - both with functional fireplaces, small corner sinks, front and side windows and a slightly pitched roof at the front, both with doors leading to large, tiny-windowed storage rooms - the front left was open, but the front right was locked with no key to be found.

"I'll take this one," selects Joanna, staring out of the window - her eyes winding up the long driveway. "The front left. It's brilliant!"

"A great choice," agrees Roger, "I'll look at the front right in the morning and see if I can open that other storage room. Very intriguing."

Roger and Joanna make their way downstairs to join Trish. She's beavering away in the living room and is lost in a sea of silk and satin.

"Mummy, Mummy!" cries Joanna. "Guess what?"

"What is it?" asks Trish, taking her foot off the sewing machine pedal and peering over her close work glasses.

"I've got two rooms!" excites Joanna, "My princess room and now, my very own playroom on the top floor, where I can put all my books and school stuff."

"Sounds brilliant, Joanna," replies Trish. "What a great idea!"

9
That's grand!

"There you go, Mr Pulton," says Beth, the red overalled telecommunications engineer has returned - proud of her achievement and knowing how appreciated this news will be. "You now have Wi-Fi!"

"That's excellent, Beth!" exclaims Roger, shaking Beth's hand and shouting up to Joanna. "Joanna, darling..."

"Yes, Daddy?" replies Joanna, leaving her bedroom and leaning over the bannister. "What is it?"

"We have Wi-Fi!" celebrates Roger, making a half-hearted attempt at holding arms aloft like a champion boxer.

"Fantastic news!" shouts Joanna, "Thank you, Beth."

"You're very welcome," loudly replies Beth, "and thank you for being so patient."

"I'm off to video-call Jenny," excites Joanna as she races up to her playroom to fire up her computer. "Bye."

Roger can hear Joanna and Jenny wittering away, as he brings his toolbox up to the top floor - determined to access the storage room in the front-right room. He sprays a little lubricant and jiggles the handle to see if it's just stuck rather than locked, but to no avail. Now armed with chisel and hammer, Roger, about to take drastic action and take the first blow, spies a small metal ring, sticking out from underneath the skirting board. There are no carpets in this room, just bare floorboards, beautifully patinated through centuries of natural ageing. He bends down and teases out the object. It's a key - larger than usual, as old keys tend to be, ornate in bow detail and simple castellated-cut working end. It glides into the lock like a hand into a perfectly fitting glove and turns with ease. "Thank goodness for that!" says Roger, aloud, semi-scolding and semi-congratulating, "...and I was about to destroy the lock!"

The door opens towards him, which is unusual, but no surprise, given its identical nature to Joanna's playroom. Roger slides his left hand around the door, feeling and fumbling for the light switch, which he finds but the bulb has either blown or is missing. Turning to his toolbox, Roger grabs his torch and shines it around the dark room like an air raid searchlight.

It's full of stuff. Some of it is instantly recognisable - lots of stacked wooden chairs, the type you might find in a church or an old school, several metal beds like old dormitory or hospital beds, stacked vertically, with their chain mattress supports sagging towards the floor and the black paint finishes tainted with rust. Several school desks - metal structures supporting basic wooden bench-seats and side-by-side wooden lidded desks with sliding brass inkwells, stacked floor to ceiling.

"How extraordinary!" remarks Roger to himself, beginning to unload the chairs for better access. "I wonder what's buried in here. Years of history, crammed into this small space that hasn't seen the light of day for years - at least thirty years, I'd say...maybe coincidental with the old lady's husband passing..."

An hour later and the front-right room is full of chairs, beds, desks, gymnasium benches, folding wooden tables, old sports equipment, various-sized boxes - some full of old parlour games, some full of odds and sods and some full of bits and bobs...possibly fixtures and fittings from the house, stretching back to medieval times!

Roger uses the vacuum cleaner to clean as he goes, sucking away years of dust, dreadlock-like cobwebs, mummified flies and dishevelled, hollow spiders. The small side window suddenly breathes life into the room as Roger runs the nozzle over it with the soft-ended attachment. A new light bulb adds the icing to the cake as the room becomes saturated with light, spilling into all corners. In the far-left corner are several mirrors, propped against each other - some large and ornate, some narrow and straightforward. On removal, Roger finds a large canvas-covered structure, almost as tall and as wide as his span, protruding a few feet from the wall. As he vacuums the dust, again with the soft-ended attachment, the dark blue canvas begins to smarten, and gold piping gleams and glistens.

"What's this?" Roger says, bemused, laying the vacuum cleaner down and trying to budge the large blue structure, "It's heavy, whatever it is!"

Roger glances to the floor to see a long castored-platform with, what appears to be, locking levers at either end. He lifts each lever with his right foot, feeling the castor wheels screech and groan, as they experience long-forgotten freedom.

Roger slowly guides the unit backwards, looking over both shoulders as he negotiates the door, trying not to bump into anything. There isn't enough space in the front-right room, so he guides the unit onto the landing, before applying the locking levers once more.

Joanna finishes another call to Jenny and leaves her room. She isn't expecting to see her Dad on the landing, especially standing in front of a huge blue and gold object - on wheels!

"What's that, Daddy?" enquires Joanna, eyeing the unit up and down.

"I have no idea!" replies Roger, shrugging his shoulders, "I found it in the storage cupboard, along with thousands of other things. Take a look. It's staggering."

Joanna enters the front-right room and is immediately taken aback, before spying some *perfect-for-her-playroom* objects! Just as she's about to ask for one of the desks, Roger manages to pull the canvas cover upwards, slowly unveiling the object beneath.

"It looks like an instrument, Daddy," remarks Joanna as she watches Roger struggle with the last few feet before gently resting the removed cover on the floor and stepping back.

"You couldn't be more right!" amazes Roger, using slightly strange English for effect, "It's a piano and not just any old piano, Joanna. It's a grand piano, in its stored vertical position!"

"A PIANO!" excites Joanna, "I've always wanted a piano, but we didn't have space in our last house, just room for my small plastic keyboard."

"This is incredible!" also excites Roger, "Let me get Jim to help assemble it into its correct position," suggests Roger, leaning over the bannister and shouting, "Jim! Please, come up to the top floor."

Jim joins Roger, and after a bit of working out and removing it from the platform, they eventually get the piano to resemble the most luxurious grand piano either has ever seen - whirling walnut veneers, gold gilt fretwork and highly polished metalwork, in dire need of buffing after years of dormancy.

"I think I've found the piano seat," shouts Joanna, struggling to lift it from the storage room, moaning and groaning with each problematic step.

"Let me help you," says Jim, grabbing the stool from Joanna, placing it by the piano and brushing the top surface with quick hand movements. Joanna immediately sits on it, opens the piano lid and begins *banging* on the ivory keys!

"I'm no musical expert," admits Roger, "but I'd say it sounds remarkably in tune!"

Joanna tinkles the keys as Roger and Jim admire the craftsmanship, trying to guess its age, until Roger discovers a metal plaque on the inside, inscribed: *Bösendorfer 90, Vienna, 1828.*

"I, too, am no music expert," adds Jim, "but looking at the construction and materials, I'd say the stool is even earlier! It looks mid-eighteenth century...1750's Georgian."

Trish appears as if lured by the sound of the Pied Piper - if the Pied Piper had been poorly playing the piano. She stops in her tracks to peruse the sight before her.

"Look, Mummy, my very own piano," cries Joanna. "My very own grand piano!"

10

Guten Tag!

At breakfast the following morning, Roger, Trish and Joanna talk about nothing else. Joanna is beside herself with excitement. She found it impossible to sleep, repeatedly dreaming of playing this grandest of pianos - the most majestic piano, fit for a king or queen...and a princess!

"Is there any chance we have to give it back to the old lady's family?" asks Joanna, fingers crossed for the answer.

"No, Joanna," replies Roger, delighted to see her face change from worry to relief.

"Are you sure, Roger?" enquires Trish, looking for reassurance, "We don't want some legal wrangling."

"The piano is now ours," confirms Roger. "Once contracts are complete and keys handed over, the house and all its contents, including the piano, in this case, become the rightful possession of the new owners - that's us!"

"The piano's too beautiful to be hidden on the top floor," suggests Trish, smiling at Joanna and sipping her coffee. "It needs to be somewhere it can be seen and admired."

"Mummy's right!" agrees Joanna, smiling back at Trish and straw-sucking another mouthful of milky tea. "The piano's much too beautiful."

"I totally agree," nods Roger, smiling at both Joanna and Trish and gulping the last of his tea. "It should take centre stage in the living room with the lake vista as the backdrop. I'll call Jim and ask if

...ne of his friends can lend a hand to bring it downstairs. It's much too heavy for us."

Jim arrives with his brother, Rob and their friend, Paul. Following brief introductions and cups of tea or coffee, they edge the piano slowly but surely, down both flights of stairs until they reach the bottom and the castored-platform comes to their rescue. Joanna records the *piano moving saga* on her phone, giggling at the confused communication: *"Your left or my left?"* - *"My right is your left"* - *"But my right's, your right!"* - *"Not when we turn the corner, then your right is my left!"* - *"Don't push"* - *"I'm not pushing!"* - *"Hang on, I've got my leg trapped!"* It's hysterical...

They push the piano into the living room. As they glide it around the bay window, in search of the best spot, they're all surprised when the piano suddenly finds its position - all three leg castors rolling into pre-pitted indents in the parquet floor!

"My goodness," declares Roger, "this is where it was positioned before and must have been for some time, judging by the depth of the indents."

"That's unbelievable," remarks Jim, "what are the chances?"

Roger retrieves the stool from the top floor. As he brings it downstairs, he sees an elegant handle at the bottom, which when turned, adjusts the stool height. Roger turns the stool upside down to admire the ingenious engineering and discovers faint antique graffiti, although it could be an ownership mark. He rubs it with his thumb. It becomes more legible and makes him stop for a second. "No, it can't be!" he remarks, quickening his step to show everyone, "Surely not!"

Joanna reads the graffiti, gouged in the wood like a penknife tree

"I think that's a seven," corrects Roger, "W.A.M 1765."

"Maybe William, something, something," suggests Jim.

"Or Wendy, something, something?" counter suggests Joanna.

"Or Wolfgang Amadeus Mozart!" responds Roger, "He was living in London in 1765!"

"Surely not!" reply Rob and Paul, "It could be anyone."

"You may be right," replies Roger, "but you never know!"

As they deliberate over the markings, the doorbell rings.

Joanna runs over and opens the door to find a strange looking gentleman. She immediately thinks he must have come from some film or theatre set, based on his *dandy* appearance - he's wearing a magnificent, bottle green velvet long jacket, ruffled slightly at the shoulder and sporting a green silk-backed collar. A cream-coloured cravat on a crisp white shirt, whose cuffs, spring flower-like from the jacket. A deep red silk waistcoat, complete with a silver-chained fob watch. Jet black trousers, tucked into knee-high, highly polished and tri-buckled, black leather boots. Shoulder-length grey, wavy hair with a floppy fringe, he keeps flicking back with his right hand to reveal piercing dark brown eyes!

"Guten tag, Fraulein!" he greets her with a deep bow, "My name is Herr Mozhoven," he continues with a German-sounding English accent, "pronounced Moats Hoe Ven. Pleased to meet you."

"Pleased to meet you, too," replies Joanna, unaccustomed to such formalities. "Are you after my Mum or Dad?"

"Are your mutter und fater around?" he asks, slipping from English into German and back again.

"DADDY!" shouts Joanna, "there's a gentleman at the door."

"Daddy's busy with Jim," interrupts Trish as she comes to the door. "Hello, Trish Pulton. How can I help you?"

"Guten tag, Frau Pulton!" he replies, again with a deep bow, "My name is Herr Mozhoven, pronounced Moats Hoe Ven."

"Hello, Mr Moats Hoe Ven," replies Trish, slightly nervous, in response to his *over-the-top* formality, repeating, "How can I help you?"

"I am ein piano teacher," replies Herr Mozhoven, looking directly into Trish's eyes, as if to peer directly into her soul and pre-read her answers, "und I am wondering if you require my services?"

"Mr Mozhoven," replies Trish, now spooked by the coincidence of his arrival, "we've just moved in, and we haven't made any decisions about such things."

"But you do have ein piano!" replies Herr Mozhoven, "Und your daughter does want to learn. Am I right?"

"That's' right, Mummy," answers Joanna, unaware of this awkward situation, "we do have a piano, and I do want to learn, and you did say I could get some lessons."

"That's right, Joanna," responds Trish, smiling uncomfortably at Herr Mozhoven, "but we don't even know Mr Mozhoven, Joanna."

"Dass is correct, Frau Pulton, excuse me!" apologises Herr Mozhoven, taking a card from his waistcoat and opening his sheet music leather case to extract two sheets of finest quality paper. "Please, take my card und two references."

Trish examines the card. It's the most elegant card she's ever seen - graced with flamboyant, gold-foiled typography and countless letters after his name. Then she glances at the references, and her mouth opens as if to say something, but no words are forthcoming. One reference carries the Music School of Vienna Crest and the other, which makes her mouth open even wider, bears the Royal Palace Crest, outlining Herr Mozhoven's *excellence* in training several royal grandsons and granddaughters. "Goodness me, Herr Mozhoven, you come highly recommended," compliments Trish, deliberately using Herr instead of Mr, to echo the formality of the references. "However, I'm not sure if we can afford you!"

"You tell me what you think is ein fair price," replies Herr Mozhoven, "und that will suffice!"

"Please, Mummy!" pleads Joanna, warming to Herr Mozhoven, "It's what the piano deserves."

"Very well, Herr Mozhoven," replies Trish, "we would love for you to teach Joanna the piano."

"Sehr gut!" replies Herr Mozhoven, retrieving the references and deep bowing again, "Very good. I shall see you tomorrow at five o'clock. Auf wiedersehen. Goodbye."

Trish closes the door, not sure if what just happened, really happened! She looks again at the card and is confused by the lack of address or contact details, but gets distracted by Joanna's exuberance and thinks nothing more about it...

11

Wax on, wax off!

"Hi, Jenny," greets Joanna, sitting on her new school desk, positioned in front of the main playroom window. It works well there because Fortuna House is north-facing, consequently without any direct, blinding or distracting sunlight at the front. "How's it going?"

"Life's not the same since you left," moans Jenny, pulling her bottom lip over her top lip and fake crying. "Just me and my stinky brother!"

"But we speak every day, sometimes three times a day," remarks Joanna, trying to cheer up her best friend. "Other than the first ten days when we had no Wi-Fi, it doesn't feel any different!"

"I suppose you're right," admits Joanna, pulling an exaggerated happy smile. "Now, tell me more about your piano."

"Well, it's funny you should ask," begins Joanna, looking left and right, as if to check the coast is clear before revealing a massive secret. "I'm having lessons! In fact, my first lesson starts in half an hour, so I haven't got long."

"That's amazing," replies Jenny, "I wish I'd kept up with my flute, but I couldn't stand my teacher...even though she supplied copious amounts of wine gums at the end of each lesson."

"Talking of teachers," continues Joanna. "Mine's a bit strange! He reminds me of an antique four-poster bed - the kind you see in stately homes..."

"What do you mean?" asks Jenny, confused by the comparison of a person with a bed.

"Well, firstly, he's old," continues Joanna, holding up her hand to reveal five fingers and pointing to her thumb, "secondly, he looks like something you don't find very often today," adds Joanna, pointing to her index finger, "thirdly, he's *flowery*! Fourthly, he's larger than life," further adds Joanna, pointing to her middle finger, then her ring finger, "and fifthly and *finally*, he's formal. He even bows when he says hello and goodbye, and he's even got papers from the palace!"

"And he's your piano teacher!" responds Jenny, giving Joanna a questioning look.

"Yep," Joanna proclaims proudly, "Herr Mozhoven, pronounced Moats Hoe Ven, the perfect piano teacher for my princess piano!"

"My Mum's calling me, Joanna," finishes Jenny. "Gotta go. Can't wait to hear all about your lesson with *Hairy Moist Oven!*"

"Herr Mozhoven!" defends Joanna, although smiling at Jenny's funny nickname, "See ya!"

Joanna waits patiently for Herr Mozhoven at the bottom of the stairs, watching the second hand revolve on the big wall clock. "One, elephant, two, elephant, three, elephant..." counts Joanna, eyes closed, trying to guess ten seconds, only to find she's either too fast or too slow. She tries a different method. "One, Mozhoven, two, Mozhoven, three, Mozhoven...ten, Mozhoven," counts Joanna, now finding her timing is impeccable! She counts for longer. She's exact again and again and again! "Unbelievable!" she thinks, just as the doorbell chimes. It's five o'clock on the dot!

"I see you've discovered the Mozhoven timing-technique," announces Herr Mozhoven, walking past Joanna and heading straight for the living room. "Dass is lesson number one."

"But, but…" fumbles Joanna, closing the door and trying to work out how he knew what she'd been doing, "…how did you know, Herr Mozhoven? I was counting in my head!"

"Ya, ya," replies Herr Mozhoven, resting his sheet music leather case on the grand piano, followed by finger-by-finger glove pulling before complete removal of his dark blue leather gloves. "We have no time to waste, Yoanna. Chop, chop!"

"My name is Joanna, Herr Mozhoven," corrects Joanna as she nestles into the piano stool, "not Yoanna!"

"Ya, ya, Yoanna, dass is what I said!" replies Herr Mozhoven, taking a tiny bejewelled gold carriage clock from his jacket and placing it on the piano, before looking at Joanna's attire, "How can you learn to play the piano when you're dressed ready for bed?"

"These are my *leggings*, Herr Mozhoven," replies Joanna, "and this is my cool top my friend, Jenny, gave me for my last birthday!"

"Pyjamas!" cries Herr Mozhoven, "Please, go und change into your best clothes, as if you're going to church."

"But this is how I go to church when I go," replies Joanna.

"Then ein party dress, please!" requests Herr Mozhoven, tutting and rolling his eyes, just like Joanna does, "We cannot start until you follow lesson number two. Smart clothes for smart piano playing - sloppy clothes for sloppy piano playing. Always."

Joanna races upstairs, changes quickly into her navy blue lace party dress, pulls on some orange tights, slips into silver pumps and runs downstairs to take her place on the stool again.

"Sehr gut!" applauds Herr Mozhoven, "Now we can start lesson three."

Joanna lifts the lid. She struggles, given its weight and length, adding, "My Dad thinks the piano may need tuning."

"Please, close the lid, Yoanna," simply says Herr Mozhoven, "I will tune it when we finish. You are not ready to touch the piano yet!"

"What do you mean?" puzzles Joanna, "How can I learn the piano without playing the piano?"

"Place your hands on the piano lid und spread your fingers as wide as you can," instructs Herr Mozhoven, ignoring Joanna's question. "Now stretch your back und hold your head completely still, looking straight-ahead."

Joanna follows his instructions as Herr Mozhoven places an old red leather-bound book on her head. "Stretch your arms as far as you can without losing the book und then bring them back in," further instructs Herr Mozhoven as he moves around Joanna like a hairdresser contemplating a suitable haircut. "Now repeat this, using the Mozhoven timing-technique for twenty minutes. Close your eyes und imagine you are playing."

Joanna concentrates - her lips moving as if in silent prayer until she completes the given task, counting aloud for the last ten seconds and concluding, "Fifty-nine, Mozhoven, stop, Mozhoven."

It is the longest Joanna has been this still - not that she has *ants in her pants,* but her mind starts typically wandering after five minutes, and she looks to do something else. These twenty minutes, however, strangely felt more like five minutes!

"Perfect, Yoanna!" congratulates Herr Mozhoven as Joanna opens her eyes and observes twenty minutes exactly on the carriage clock. "That concludes lesson number three: *Posture* und today's lesson. Please, practise this. Now you can leave while I tune this wonderful piano."

Joanna is shell-shocked. She hasn't played a single note, but somehow feels like she's played an entire symphony! Leaving the door slightly ajar, Joanna watches Herr Mozhoven tune the piano.

He takes a small bow-tied silk pouch from his jacket breast pocket, lays it on the piano and unwraps it to reveal a large brass key, large enough to insert four fingers, a dark grey tuning fork and a gold telescopic baton. Taking his position at the keyboard, Herr Mozhoven picks up the baton with his right hand, extends it with his left hand and begins silently conducting - swaying his head side to side as he repeatedly flicks his floppy fringe, intermittently striking a piano key with his left index finger then immediately picking up the tuning fork, tapping it on the piano then laying it down. He then picks up the large brass key, leaning into the piano and tweaking something inside, while still conducting with his other hand as if in some deep trance! Twenty minutes later, Herr Mozhoven places the items back in the pouch, rewraps it, reties the bow, then replaces it back in his jacket breast pocket and leaves quietly.

Joanna makes sure he doesn't see her and is completely mesmerised by the whole experience.

'How was your piano lesson with Herr Mozhoven?" asks Roger, carrying a stack of black and white tiles across the hallway and looking at Joanna's smart blue dress. "Or have you been to a party?"

'The lesson was unbelievable, Daddy!" replies Joanna, watching her Dad disappear upstairs. "Absolutely unbelievable!"

12

Your carriage awaits, Ma'am!

"...he was like a mad wizard, Jenny!" enthuses Joanna, randomly waving a gigantic rubber-ended white pencil to mimic Herr Mozhoven's piano tuning, before embellishing, "And his eyes were bright orange as if they were on fire and sparks were flying from his baton..."

"You're joking!" responds Jenny, not knowing whether to believe Joanna or not. "Weren't you scared?"

"A little," replies Joanna, leaning closer to the camera, "but there *is* something magical about him. I can't wait for my next lesson to see what he's going to do next!"

There's a knock at the door. "Joanna, darling," begins Roger, "can you say goodbye to Jenny and come and have some lunch."

"Bye, Jenny," sighs Joanna, closing her computer and exiting her playroom to find her Dad closing his study door - his black hair speckled in *dove grey* and ageing him by ten years. "Goodness, Daddy, have you seen your hair?"

"I'm a rock 'n' roller painter!" jokes Roger, pretending to roller paint like John Travolta with high-pitched singing, "Ha, ha, ha, ha, stayin' alive, stayin' alive!"

Joanna and Roger make their way downstairs, planning lunch.

"I fancy pesto-pasta with a little grated cheese," suggests Joanna, licking her lips and rubbing her stomach.

"Sounds like a good plan," agrees Roger as they reach the ground floor and find Trish in the dining room, hand stitching the hems on her recently finished long silk deep purple drapes. "Pesto-pasta good for you, too, Trish?"

"Mmm, bellisimo!" replies Trish, in her best Italian accent and blowing a pinched-finger kiss. "Sounza goood!"

Fifteen minutes later and Roger, Trish and Joanna are enjoying the culinary miracle of jarred pesto, poured onto twelve-minute boiled pasta and sprinkled with parmesan cheese and cracked black pepper!

"I think I need a break from painting this afternoon," states Roger. "I think I'll go down to the stables and make a start there."

"Now that's a big job, Darling!" adds Trish. "Why don't you take Joanna with you?"

"Oooh, yes, please," excites Joanna, "I'd love to come and help!"

"Brilliant!" replies Roger, "I suggest you wear old clothes - it's going to be very dirty and dusty!"

Joanna wolfs her remaining fusilli and runs upstairs to change into old jeans, a yellow shirt she's not very fond of and a brown tracksuit top, bought for her at *5-6 years,* but still *fitting* - riding high on both her waist and arms.

Roger and Joanna leave by the front door and head diagonally right towards the stables. Joanna suddenly stops, "Hang on a sec, Daddy," she shouts, "I just need to get something!"

Joanna returns, clutching Herr Mozhoven's red leather-bound book.

"What's that?" enquires Roger, taking the book from Joanna and studying it.

"It's my *posture* book!" replies Joanna, "Herr Mozhoven gave it to me yesterday, to help me play the piano!"

"The History of Little Goody Two-Shoes," reads Roger, intrigued as to its use and by its age, "Wow! It's a first edition, published in 1765. If I remember rightly, it's like the Cinderella story, but instead of a glass slipper, it's about an orphan with only one shoe who's given two by some rich guy. It makes her very happy. She tells everyone, becomes a teacher, ends up marrying a rich widower and lives happily ever after!"

"What a bizarre story, Daddy!" replies Joanna, looking down at her *two-shoes* and thinking of the endless pairs she has in her wardrobe, before continuing, "Herr Mozhoven says the book will improve my posture," informs Joanna, taking back the book. "Here, let me show you."

Joanna places the book on her head, *stretches* her back and points her perfectly still head, straight-ahead. She catches the book twice as it falls but then manages to balance it in position. Anyone watching could be forgiven for mistaking her for a *seed-sower,* as she begins to *play* the piano, left and right as far as she can reach, fingers alternating and moving rapidly up and down...*sowing the seed*, then back to begin again - *refilling the seed.* "See, Daddy?" shouts Joanna, working hard not to spill the book. "Posture!"

"Very good, Joanna," says Roger, walking by her side - his trainers still *slapping* as they edge down the gravel path and reach the stableyard...adding, much to Joanna's groaning, "Herr Mozhoven seems to be sowing all the right seeds!"

Walking through a large arch carved into a substantial tile-topped wall, Joanna and Roger enter the stableyard with its fully encompassing left and right stables and sizeable central barn at the far end. It is topped with an elegant, bright blue clock faced turret, displaying golden numbers and golden hands, showing the wrong time. The stableyard and arch are large enough to accept a four-horse-drawn carriage and provide a generous turning circle. The cobbles underfoot are well-weathered and aged, through centuries of continuous use.

"This is magical, Daddy," exclaims Joanna, imagining horses neighing and carriages being prepared. "Like a fairy tale!"

"This is yester-year's garage!" replies Roger, "Before the days of gas-guzzling motorcars and taken-for-granted quick trips to the supermarket!"

Roger and Joanna go from stable to stable, starting near left and moving clockwise. They open each slightly jaded, bottle green-coloured door, significantly protected by the cantilevered roof. Some nameplates remain, carelessly painted in gold paint - a few misjudged with last letters, annoyingly squeezed in.

"Hey look, Daddy," shouts Joanna, "there's one here called *Jenny!*"

"How funny!" remarks Roger, "Especially when all the others seem to be flowers - Dandelion, Daisy, Petunia, Primrose, Foxglove and Hollyhock!"

Most of the stables have remnants of straw, wall hanging old tack, worn bristled brooms, rusty shovels and once sharp pitchforks. Joanna helps Roger collect all the items and sweep the left-hand stables, ready for hosing down.

"Let's leave the right-hand stables for later and have a look in the barn," decides Roger, in need of a rest, as he wipes the sweat from his brow.

Roger heaves open the large barn door - right side first, then left. Joanna joins him. The middle section of the barn is open to the roof, where two glass-paned skylights shed light into an otherwise gloomy area. Unfortunately, the roof shows signs of damage as slithers of sky, shine through thin slits like daylight stars. The left and right sections of the barn have tongue and groove, panelled dividing walls and safety railed mezzanine floors, accessed via wooden step ladders.

"Do you think there will be any mice, Daddy?" frets Joanna as they peer behind the left-section wall.

"Surely, not!" replies Roger, taking Joanna's hand and hoping this to be true. "Now let's see what we have here..."

Roger carefully pulls back a loose-fitting dust sheet to reveal a deep red antique horse carriage. Horse connecting bars stooped to the floor. Cartwheels buckled and spoke-broken. Carriage-lamps, singular - one clearly missing. Door windows, stained and occasionally cracked.

"It's like Cinderella's carriage!" Joanna sighs in a dreamy voice.

"You mean the old pumpkin before the Fairy Godmother casts her spell!" jests Roger, opening the carriage door and checking no animals are nesting inside, then standing to attention like an old-fashioned footman and announcing, "Your carriage awaits, Ma'am. Please, step this way!"

"Thank you, Jeeves!" replies Joanna, taking Roger's outstretched hand to steady herself, stepping onto the footplate and into the carriage. "Home, James - and don't spare the horses!"

13

Close your eyes and open your ears!

"...I'll give it some thought," replies Roger, trying to be positive, "but it really has seen better days!"

"I'll help," enthuses Joanna, grabbing an old broom and brushing the sides with little effect, "we may not be able to get it rolling again, Daddy, but it could be a pretend princess carriage! Somewhere my friends and I can play and make-believe."

"Thinking about it..." responds Roger, taking his tape measure from his pocket and measuring one of the identically-sized cartwheels, "...36 inches! Perhaps it might be easy to repair - it's amazing what you can get on the internet nowadays, but I'm not promising anything."

"Roger...Joanna," calls Trish as she enters the barn, balancing three drinks on a bright red plastic tray, "Tea's up! I thought you might like a break and a..." Trish pauses for effect as she reaches into her coat pocket, "...chocolate biscuit!"

"You're a star!" declares Roger, taking a mug and three biscuits!

"Thank you, Mummy!" replies Joanna, taking her apple juice carton, ripping off the miniature straw and piercing the tiny circular foil, "Come and look at this..." she insists, grabbing Trish by the hand as Trish takes her coffee and lays down the tray, "I've got something amazing to show you!"

"Wow!" exclaims Trish, spying the carriage, "What a brilliant thing!"

"Daddy says he's going to repair it!" says Joanna excitedly, knowing she's pushing her luck.

"I made no promises!" replies Roger loudly, overhearing Joanna's wishful thinking as he ventures over to the right section. "Hey

Joanna, Trish, come and look over here - there's another sheet-covered thing!"

Trish and Joanna hurry over - Joanna faster than Trish.

Roger pulls back the loose-fitting sheet to reveal a vintage Edwardian motorcar - open-topped and splendid, but completely clapped-out. The tyres are thin, large, wire-spoked and flat. The front grille is wire-meshed, with the starter crank handle missing. The headlights are big, bold, brass and broken. In the rear, which is higher than the front, the seats are buttoned red-leathered, faded and torn. There is a huge horn - rubber ballooned, bugle-shaped and bent!

"Now that's more like it!" excites Roger - a secret petrolhead, eager to put his engineering skills to good use. "Imagine getting this running, Trish - and going for picnics on sunny afternoons..."

"What about me?" cries Joanna, honking the *honk-less* horn and raising her eyebrows like a big question mark.

"Of course, you'd come too," replies Trish, "a picnic wouldn't be a picnic without you!"

Roger, Trish and Joanna sit in the car - Joanna in the driving seat of course. They make old-fashioned car noises and pretend they're on the way back from the races. All very silly, but great fun!

"Right!" announces Trish, opening the door and climbing down, "As much as I would love to stay and take *a trip to the seaside*, I need to finish something in the house."

Roger and Joanna watch Trish disappear from the stableyard, then each grabs a broom and begin sweeping the barn. Soon, however, there is a change in the weather...

"Looks like rain," observes Roger, stepping out to view the darkening clouds, "and the wind's picking up."

Roger moves an old wooden bench for Joanna to sit on, just as the rain begins to fall. "Why don't you watch the rain, Joanna," suggests Roger, sensing she's losing steam, "while I carry on sweeping."

Joanna sits, staring at this amazing scene - contented and inspired…although she wishes Jenny was there to enjoy it with her!

The rain starts to fall more heavily, and the wind begins to blow harder. Joanna closes her eyes to listen to the previously silent setting - the rain on the tiles, making *pitter-patter* sounds, while the rain on the skylight *pings*…both sounds are speeding up and slowing down, getting louder and quieter as the weather changes pace. A big drip begins hitting the inside of an old metal bathtub, ticking like the second hand of a noisy clock and echoing in the enclosed shape. A far stable door joins in, squeaking as its rusty hinge opens, crash-banging as it catches the wind, then thrown back like a beaten drum, repeating, repeating. Leaf-filled trees swish and sway, rustling like dried peas in an old tin. Even Roger's regular sweeping makes a sound similar to a snare drum, acting as the backbone and backbeat. Individually, the sounds are no particularly special, but together, their combination and rhythm are undeniably distinctive, creating a unique symphony!

Joanna can't help daydreaming how nature is playing its very own piano!

Joanna opens her eyes, distracted by Roger knocking over a solitary piece of wood. She looks at her watch and suddenly remembers, "Daddy, I've got to go!" she shouts, realising she's going to get wet, "I've got seven minutes to get back to the house, change into something smart and be ready for Herr Mozhoven at five o'clock!"

"You better get your skates on, Joanna!" encourages Roger, "You can't keep Herr Mozhoven waiting."

Joanna doesn't know how she did it, but she gets back to the house, is smartly dressed in a red smock dress and leaving her bedroom just as the doorbell chimes.

"I've got it, Mummy!" she shouts, double-stair jumping downstairs and opening the door, "Hello, Herr Mozhoven."

"Ein minute past five, Yoanna! Lesson number five: *Tardiness!*" states Herr Mozhoven, standing in the rain without an umbrella, but wearing the most amazing hat - a hat resembling a purple top hat with gold skirted ribbon, but with an extra-large dished brim, collecting rainwater and shooting it out the back via a specially formed shoot. "Ein pianist cannot be tardy, or they fall behind the beat und mess up the rhythm!"

"Do you mean lateness?" asks Joanna, unfamiliar with the word *tardy*.

"Ya, lateness," replies Herr Mozhoven. "Now let's get started on lesson number six."

"But you've missed out lesson number four!" points out Joanna, still fascinated by Herr Mozhoven's hat, as he removes it and places it on the hall chair.

"You have already completed lesson number four," replies Herr Mozhoven.

"I haven't," replies Joanna, "I would definitely remember!"

"You completed lesson number four in the barn," replies Herr Mozhoven, "not more than thirty minutes ago."

"You mean when I was listening to the weather?" answers Joanna.

"Exactly, Yoanna!" says Herr Mozhoven, "There is music in everything und sometimes you have to *close your eyes* und *open your ears* to hear it."

"As if nature's playing its own piano!" adds Joanna, articulately - wondering when and how Herr Mozhoven would have seen her.

"Exactly, Yoanna! Lesson number four: *Music is everywhere!*" replies Herr Mozhoven. "Now follow me to the piano und we can begin lesson number six. Chop, chop!"

"Are you left or right-handed?" asks Herr Mozhoven as he reaches into his jacket breast pocket - pulling out a cream-coloured parchment scroll with intricately turned gold ends, two parrot feathers - one red and one green and what looks like a pirate's black eyepatch.

"I'm a lefty!" replies Joanna, air writing with her left hand.

"Ah, *bass* handed!" responds Herr Mozhoven, taking Joanna's hand and examining her fingers - pulling them and checking for straightness, "From now on..." continues Herr Mozhoven, grabbing her right hand and examining it in the same way, "...you are both! Lesson number six: *Ambidexterity!*"

"My friend, Jenny, can write with both hands," replies Joanna, now examining her hands like Herr Mozhoven.

"You are neither left nor right..." Herr Mozhoven continues uninterested with Jenny's party trick as he stands directly behind Joanna, "...you are *bass* und *treble* - in everything you do, think und are. Your whole left side is *bass!*" he declares, placing his *bass* hand on Joanna's *bass* shoulder, "Und your whole right side is *treble!*" he finishes, placing his *treble* hand on Joanna's *treble* shoulder.

"*Bass!*" repeats Joanna, holding up her left hand, "*Treble!*" adds Joanna, holding up her right hand.

"Perfect, Yoanna!" replies Herr Mozhoven as he moves back to the side of the piano, picking up the scroll and unrolling it onto the piano lid. The scroll has a five-line stave running its entire length. Then Herr Mozhoven hands her a red feather, which Joanna can see now is an old-fashioned quill, followed by the patch, saying, "Red is *bass* und green is *treble!* Place the patch over your *treble* eye und hold the red feather in your *bass* hand."

"Ah, me hearties!" jokes Joanna, unable to help herself as she follows Herr Mozhoven's instructions, quickly realising he isn't amused!

"You will attempt the *bass* hand first..." continues Herr Mozhoven, taking out his bejewelled gold carriage clock and placing it on the piano, "...for five minutes. Write your name - only thinking und looking with your *bass* eye...concentrating on every *bass* hand movement. Begin."

Joanna finds it difficult at first as she struggles with judging depth and writing with a quill - a quill she's never written with before, a quill that never seems to run out! However, after five minutes, everything seems natural, and her name looks legible and familiar.

"Sehr gut!" applauds Herr Mozhoven, rolling and unrolling the scroll to erase Joanna's repeated name magically. "Now for something more challenging. Repeat the exercise using this green *treble* feather und place the patch over your *bass* eye."

Joanna finds this nearly impossible - not just judging depth and quill-writing, but writing with her right hand or rather her *treble* hand. She uses extra concentration, and after five minutes, to her amazement, everything seems as natural, as legible and as familiar as her *bass* hand!

"Sehr gut!" applauds Herr Mozhoven, again rolling and unrolling the scroll to magically erase Joanna's repeated name, before handing back the red feather. "Now no patch! *Bass* und *treble* working in harmony - true *Ambidexterity!*"

Joanna struggles again, but the harder she concentrates, the more her *bass* eye controls her *bass* hand and the more her *treble* eye controls her *treble* hand! She can't help but applaud herself,

"Look, Herr Mozhoven, I'm doing it! I'm writing my name at the same time - using my *bass* and *treble* hands!

"Sehr gut!" replies Herr Mozhoven, "Now for lesson number seven!"

Usually, Joanna would be rolling her eyes and tutting at this point, complaining - *Not another lesson!* Or *Why can't I start playing now? Surely, I'm ready!* But not this time - Joanna is enjoying the lessons, and everything seems to make perfect sense!

"Lesson number seven..." announces Herr Mozhoven, collecting the feathers and patch and placing them on the piano, ready for Joanna to use, "...is: *Mnemonics!*"

"*Mnemonics!*" repeats Joanna, "We learnt about these at school. It's when you make a phrase from letters so that you can remember more easily!"

"Exactly, Yoanna." responds Herr Mozhoven, taking a green card from his jacket breast pocket, "Put the patch on your *bass* eye und read this green card. What is green?"

"*Treble!*" replies Joanna, applying the patch and taking the green card.

"*Treble* is everything dass side of centre," adds Herr Mozhoven, pointing to a blue, centrally-mounted sapphire on the piano and hand gesturing *away* from him, "where the centre is *middle C*."

"**E**very **F**ancy **G**irl **A**lways **B**oils **C**racking **D**evilled **E**ggs **F**irst," reads Joanna, immediately remembering a wedding she was dragged to, where curried eggs - which she absolutely detests, kept being referred to as *devilled eggs!*

"Turn the card over, Yoanna!" instructs Herr Mozhoven, "You will see this mnemonic broken down into two further mnemonics. Read each one."

"Four spaces: **F**ancy **A**lways **C**racking **E**ggs!" reads Joanna, "Five lines: **E**very **G**irl **B**oils **D**evilled **F**irst!"

"Now stand up und march around the room, repeating both sides of the card for five minutes," instructs Herr Mozhoven, tapping the top of the piano to add rhythm to her recital, "as if you're marching und saying each word on each step!"

At first, Joanna feels self-conscious but quickly imagines herself dressed as an eye-patched soldier, marching outside the palace - shouting each word and saluting after each mnemonic.

"Sehr gut!" applauds Herr Mozhoven, taking a red card from his jacket breast pocket, "Now put the patch on your *treble* eye und read this red card. What is red?"

"*Bass!*" replies Joanna, applying the patch and taking the red card.

"*Bass* is everything this side of centre," adds Herr Mozhoven, pointing to the blue sapphire again and hand gesturing *towards* him, again adding, "Where centre is *middle C.*"

"**G**ood **A**ustrian **B**ourgeois **C**hefs **D**o **E**at **F**ine **G**oulash **A**lso," reads Joanna, this time remembering how much she loves goulash and how Jenny's Mum always makes it!"

"Again, turn the card over, Yoanna!" instructs Herr Mozhoven, "You will see *this* mnemonic broken down into two further mnemonics. Read each one."

"Four spaces: **A**ustrian **C**hefs **E**at **G**oulash!" reads Joanna, "Five lines: **G**ood **B**ourgeois **D**o **F**ine **A**lso!"

"Und again, march und repeat!" instructs Herr Mozhoven, delighted that Joanna is adding her own twists!

Joanna finishes, removes the patch and sits at the piano again.

"Keep the cards und feathers und patch und practise *Ambidexterity* und *Mnemonics*, Yoanna!" encourages Herr

Mozhoven, "Now we put them into use in lesson number eight: *Reading Music!*"

Herr Mozhoven unrolls the scroll again. The five-line stave has disappeared, magically replaced by two five-line staves which are spaced apart with nine elliptical black dots on each stave, staggered and ascending left to right and an extra black dot with a line through - *middle C* - placed below the bottom line on the top stave and above the top line on the bottom stave.

"Pick up the green feather," instructs Herr Mozhoven. "What is green?"

"*Treble!*" replies Joanna, pleased she's keeping up and remembering everything.

"Now use your *treble* mnemonics," says Herr Mozhoven, pointing to the top notes, "und give each note the correct letter."

"**E**very **F**ancy **G**irl **A**lways **B**oils **C**racking **D**evilled **E**ggs **F**irst," recites Joanna, labelling each note correctly and double-checking, "Four spaces: **F**ancy **A**lways **C**racking **E**ggs - Five lines: **E**very **G**irl **B**oils **D**evilled **F**irst!"

Sehr gut!" applauds Herr Mozhoven, "Now pick up the red feather. What is red?"

"*Bass!*" replies Joanna, answering before he's finished.

"Now use your *bass* mnemonics," says Herr Mozhoven, pointing to the bottom notes, "und give each note the correct letter."

"**G**ood **A**ustrian **B**ourgeois **C**hefs **D**o **E**at **F**ine **G**oulash **A**lso," recites Joanna, labelling each note correctly and double-checking, "Four spaces: **A**ustrian **C**hefs **E**at **G**oulash - Five lines: **G**ood **B**ourgeois **D**o **F**ine **A**lso!"

"Sehr gut, Joanna, sehr gut!" applauds Herr Mozhoven, "That is lesson number eight: *Reading Music...*or at least the basics!"

15

The *greenhouse.* Or is it the *treblehouse?*

"...what's a *Bourgeois chef* when they're at home?" asks Jenny, pleased with her pronunciation, delighted Joanna has called her again, "I've never heard of one before."

"My Mum says, *Bourgeois* is another description for *middle-class*," replies Joanna, "so I'm presuming a *Bourgeois chef* is a *middle-class* chef, whatever that means!"

"My Mum says we're *middle-class!*" responds Jenny, "But her Mum, my Nan, was born *lower-class!*"

"Well, whoever lived in Fortuna House," suggests Joanna, "must have been *upper-class* with horse-drawn carriages and posh motorcars!"

"My Mum says we're all born wearing the same birthday suit!" adds Jenny, "So we should always treat each other the same."

"Exactly, Jenny," replies Joanna. "Take everyone at face value!"

"Unless you don't like them!" jokes Jenny, pinching her nose with one hand and wafting the air with the other, "Like stinky boys!"

"Or Mr Knapton!" adds Joanna, giggling and nodding, "...who used to make us run around the sports field in the pouring rain!"

"Exactly!" replies Jenny, then changing the subject, "How many *likes* have you had on *Joanna Jaws?* I've had 142 on mine!"

"I haven't looked recently," replies Joanna - impressed with Jenny's score, "last time I looked, it was up to 96!"

"When do you start school?" asks Jenny, sighing heavily at the thought, "We start three weeks on Monday."

"The same," replies Joanna as a small bell rings and a black disc *flips* to white, under *KITCHEN*, in the antique *calling system* on her playroom wall, "Oh look, *Kitchen's calling!* My Dad and Jim fixed the Victorian servant's bell system, so now we can contact each other without shouting."

"We just text or phone each other." adds Jenny, "If *we* want someone!"

"This is quite cool though, Jenny." informs Joanna, "A few rooms even have a telephone attached!"

"Bring me more tea!" trills Jenny, in her poshest voice, pretending to sip tea with her *pinky* outstretched, "and some of those freshly baked *sc'own'es!*

"You mean *sc'on'es!*" replies Joanna, in *her* poshest voice. "Sorry Jenny, I'd better go. Stinky boy, boy!"

Joanna runs downstairs, rollercoastering Snonkey down the bannisters - occasionally making him fly like a cannonball, shot from a funfair cannon, as one bannister ends and another bannister begins. She bounds into the kitchen to find Trish.

"Just wondering if you could take this mug of tea to Jim," Trish asks nicely, handing Joanna a large mug, "and can you manage some Garibaldis - Jim loves them! He's in the greenhouse."

"Greenhouse, you say?" says Joanna, placing Snonkey under her arm and heading for the back door, "Sure, Mummy, I'll take the tea and biscuits to Jim...in the *treblehouse!*"

"Thanks, Pet," says Jim, opening the greenhouse door and clearing a space on the wooden bench table, "Oooh, Garibaldis - my favourite!"

"You're very welcome, Jim," replies Joanna, pulling Snonkey from under her arm, "I like Garibaldis too!"

"Where're my manners!" says Jim, reaching for the packet and offering Joanna a biscuit, "And would your friend like one too?"

"You mean, Snonkey?" replies Joanna, whispering Jim's offer into Snonkey's ear, "Snonkey says: *No thank you, he prefers Bourbons!*"

"Snonkey, you say!" says Jim, laughing at Snonkey's reply, "That reminds me of one of my girls' cuddly toys - a big blue hippopotamus, she called *Blippo!*"

"I didn't know you had girls," replies Joanna. "Are any of them my age?"

"Goodness me, no, not now!" replies Jim, shaking his head, "They're all grown up. Bethany's 25, Bridgit's 22 and Bonnie's 19!"

"Wow! Three girls," exclaims Joanna, "and all with names beginning with *B!*"

"That's right!" nods Jim, sipping his tea and grabbing another Garibaldi, "All names beginning with *B*, all born on a Sunday evening, all bonny and blithe!"

"Is that why you called Bonnie, Bonnie?" asks Joanna, looking at Jim and trying to picture his daughters - given his balding head, weather-worn wrinkles and slight potbelly!

"One of the reasons!" replies Jim, "But she was such a bundle of baby fat when she was born, it just seemed to suit her!"

"And where are they now?" enquires Joanna, also grabbing another Garibaldi.

"Let me show you a picture," responds Jim, putting on his spectacles, reaching into his back pocket for his wallet, opening it and taking out a dog-eared photo. "As you can see, this was taken a few years ago - about three years ago...but this is Bethany," he says, pointing to a tall girl with long brown hair, swept into a high ponytail, she's a lawyer now, working in Manchester. This is Brigit," he says, now pointing to a girl with fair hair and sporting bright red lipstick, "she's a nurse and lives in Leeds. And this is Bonnie," he says, finally pointing to the smaller of the three girls – she's laughing hysterically and has brown hair, tied in blue-bowed bunches, "she's a student at Liverpool University, studying to be a fashion designer."

"A fashion designer!" repeats Joanna, "I'd love to be a fashion designer. That or a baker or a photographer…or an interior designer!"

"Bethany always wanted to be a baker," replies Jim, replacing the photo in his wallet and back into his back pocket, "and now she's a high-flying lawyer!"

"So, what are you working on in here?" asks Joanna, walking down the smooth-rippled central path.

"Just fixing some glass and woodwork," replies Jim, following Joanna along the path, "and then your Dad wants me to make some potting tables and a couple of shelving units for seedlings."

"What's this?" asks Joanna, spying a dark wooden box under one of the bench tables as she reaches down and pulls it out by its old leather handle.

"Not sure," replies Jim, helping Joanna lift the box onto the bench, "I haven't seen it before."

Jim finds an old rag and wipes the top surface. There are initials W.M, amateurishly painted in black paint. The box is about 100 centimetres long, 30 centimetres deep and no more than 7 centimetres thick, with brass catches. Jim opens one catch, while Joanna opens the other, then opening the lid together. Inside are three brass objects, similar in appearance, but different sizes –

"I'm not a hundred per cent certain," begins Jim, "but I'd say this is an antique seed-planting kit, full of *seed-dibblers!*"

"Looks like it belongs to the three bears." jokes Joanna, "There's Papa Bear, Mama Bear and Baby Bear!"

"You're right, Joanna - or should I say *Goldilocks!*" remarks Jim, taking out the largest *seed-dibbler*, "When I say *seed-planting*, I mean a device for accurately spacing trees and plants. I'd say this large one is for spacing *trees*," he continues, loosening a nut and sliding apart the telescopic rods. "See the markings on the side?"

"Oh, yes!" responds Joanna, staring at the well-worn engraved markings, "Five-foot, six-foot...up to nine-foot."

"And see the two downwards-pointing brass fingers at each end?" says Jim, pointing left and right.

"Yep!" simply says, Joanna.

"Those are the six-inch *dibblers* that push into the ground, to make holes, into which you plant the seeds!" informs Jim, closing the telescopic rods, replacing it and pulling out the next size. "This one goes from two to five-foot," Jim shows Joanna before replacing it and taking out the smallest size, "and this one goes from 6 inches to two feet, but you can add more dibblers - looks like up to five fingers."

"It's ingenious!" remarks Joanna as they close the box, "Do you need this now?"

"No, Pet," replies Jim, "I've got plenty to get on with."

"I want to show my Mum and Dad and my friend, Jenny!" says Joanna, holding the box by its leather handle and clutching Snonkey in her other hand, "Thanks Jim...and thanks for our chat."

"No, thank you, Joanna, it was a real treat," replies Jim, "and thank you for the tea and Garibaldis!"

16

Finally, lesson number nine!

After her visit to the greenhouse, Joanna spends two hours - on and off, of course, practising *Ambidexterity* and *Mnemonics*, pretending to be a lady pirate called *Captain Jo an' 'er Parrot*...sailing the Caribbean and stealing gold and silver from any passing ship with her faithful red and green parrot, or at least its feathers, perched on her shoulder!

Joanna makes sure she's smartly dressed and standing by the front door by five to five o'clock. She watches the clock, and just as it strikes five o'clock, she opens the door to find Herr Mozhoven with his index finger outstretched - two inches from the doorbell!

"Hi, Herr Mozhoven," greets Joanna, adding a small curtsy, "Please, do come in."

"I like your punctuality." replies Herr Mozhoven, "It's about time!"

"Great joke, Herr Mozhoven and a great red coat!" compliments Joanna, observing Herr Mozhoven's same-styled coat to his bottle green one. "It's very *bass!*"

"Und I like your bright *treble* dress!" replies Herr Mozhoven, smiling, "Let's start lesson number nine."

"What's lesson number nine?" asks Joanna as she takes her position at the piano, "I really hope I get to play today."

"Lesson number nine is...*Playing!*" announces Herr Mozhoven, pausing for effect, before cracking a wry smile and watching Joanna's face light up with excitement. "Lift the lid und we will begin!"

Joanna warms up by playing the *Mnemonic* notes, initially with her *treble* hand, going up and away from *middle C*: **E**very **F**ancy **G**irl **A**lways **B**oils **C**racking **D**evilled **E**ggs **F**irst, then down again, followed by her *bass* hand, going up and towards *middle C*: **G**ood **A**ustrian **B**ourgeois **C**hefs **D**o **E**at **F**ine **G**oulash **A**lso, then down again, finally followed by both *bass* and *treble* hands together, going towards and away from *middle C*, at the same time.

The sound of the piano reverberates around the room and tingles through Joanna's fingers - up her arms and across to the back of her neck, making goose-pimpled hairs stand on end. Each note strike, positively feeding back and filling Joanna with an immense sense of achievement. Of course, Joanna makes mistakes - she's only human after all, but these mistakes become less and less as if the piano is helping her to self-correct.

"Sehr gut!" applauds Herr Mozhoven, "You are getting the hang of it, Yoanna."

"Thank you, Herr Mozhoven," replies Joanna, taking a breather as she stretches interlocked fingers and rolls her head side to side, "this is the most beautiful piano to play!"

"Now you are ready to play a tune!" declares Herr Mozhoven, opening his leather case and taking out a music book, "This book is perfect for beginners like you."

Herr Mozhoven hands Joanna the book. She holds her *very first music book* lightly in her fingertips, afraid of marking it - even with fingerprints...wishing she was wearing white gloves like a museum archivist, handling a rare and precious artefact! Joanna studies the front cover: *Tunes to Take You Back - simple piano pieces through the ages*. It's printed in a red and gold frilly font and illustrated with hand-painted drawings, depicting different fashions and charting changing times - from wonderful *wig-*

wearing women to Herr Mozhoven *lookalikes*, to bowler-hatted *suits* and even *smart-casual* blazers and jeans. Joanna thinks it's the best thing since sliced bread!

Joanna opens the cover to see her name already beautifully inscribed in *This book belongs to:* along with today's date. "Thank you, Herr Mozhoven," says Joanna, giving Herr Mozhoven her biggest smile, "I love it!"

"Ya, ya, Yoanna!" dismisses Herr Mozhoven, trying not to be sentimental, "Turn to page six, to the tune: *Women - we salute you*, ein simple tune from the Second World War."

"What's it about?" asks Joanna, turning to the correct page, placing the book in the piano stand and tucking it behind the small brass fingers.

"Millions of men went to fight und left women to keep everything going at home - from farming to manufacturing und everything else. This tune *salutes* this contribution und marks these big steps taken for the *modern woman*."

Herr Mozhoven pulls a metal tube from his inside jacket waist pocket. Now, Joanna believes Herr Mozhoven must have borrowed his jackets from a magician - a magician who can magically produce doves, rabbits, bunches of flowers and never-ending ribbons! The tube is about 45 centimetres long, 10 centimetres in diameter and has a metal screw top. Herr Mozhoven unscrews the lid, places it on the piano, shakes the tube upside down and produces a brass-rodded contraption.

"What's that?" asks Joanna, intrigued yet again by Herr Mozhoven.

"This is my chair!" replies Herr Mozhoven as he places the tube on the piano and expands the contraption, making a small brass stool with red canvas seat - the same red colour as his red jacket and held taut, as he tightens a central nut underneath. "I have to sit next to you, to help you with the notes!"

Note by note, Herr Mozhoven teaches the tune to Joanna. It has a celebratory feel with slight marching rhythm, possibly and - as Joanna thinks - purposefully, describing the military precision and repetitive jobs these women often fulfilled.

As they reach the sixth bar, Joanna is listening carefully and watching Herr Mozhoven play the notes, while she rubs her fingers along the underside of the piano. Then, like discovering discarded chewing gum, unceremoniously and lazily stuck to the underside of a table, Joanna finds two small levers, spaced about 40 centimetres apart.

"Herr Mozhoven!" interrupts Joanna, much to his annoyance, "What are these levers?"

"Don't touch them!" orders Herr Mozhoven...but as ten-year-old kids do, when they're told not to do something they want to do, Joanna pushes the levers anyway.

There's a clockwork sound. At either end of the keyboard, two covers slide sideways into the piano cabinet, revealing a lush red enamel-topped key to the far-left *bass* and a deep green enamel-topped key to the far-right *treble!*

Joanna peers left and right and then to the floor, expecting Herr Mozhoven to tell her off.

"This shouldn't happen!" states Herr Mozhoven, adding, "This is the *Bösendorfer 90* - the only piano in the world to have these extra keys...built in Vienna in 1828 to commemorate Ludwig van Beethoven's death in 1827. Other grand pianos have 88 keys und only a few pieces of music require one or other of these extra keys...und never both. As such, only one extra key can be accessed at any one time!"

"Have I broken it?" asks Joanna, sheepishly.

"I'm sure it wasn't you," reassures Herr Mozhoven. "It must have happened over time."

Herr Mozhoven reaches over with his *bass* hand and presses the red key. Joanna has never heard anything like it before - the bassist, lowest, deepest, heaviest note she's ever heard. It travels to the centre of her body and shakes her internal organs like a good spring clean! Then Herr Mozhoven reaches over with his *treble* hand and presses the green key. Again, Joanna has never heard anything like it before - it sounds as though angels and cherubs have started singing and the bird's morning chorus has joined in, as the treble-ist, highest, shrillest, tightest note rings-out, flicking her eardrums like an annoying schoolboy, intent on disturbing the boy in front!

"These are the most amazing sounds," adds Herr Mozhoven, "...but they must never be played together!"

"You can't, Herr Mozhoven!" jests Joanna, "Unless you have really long arms!"

"No, seriously, Yoanna!" says Herr Mozhoven, giving her a stern look, "You must promise, you will never try to play them together."

"I promise." says Joanna, crossing her fingers between her legs and out of sight, "I promise!"

Herr Mozhoven pulls the levers back - the extra key covers return, in the same clockwork manner with which they opened.

17

Now, what did Herr Mozhoven say!

"Walk up and down, Joanna," requests Trish, gesturing with her finger like she can't wave properly, "and do a twirl. Show Daddy how smart you look!"

"Do I have to?" replies Joanna, feeling like an over-groomed dog at Crufts, parading in front of the judges - just wanting to lie down and sleep, "It's just a school uniform!"

"You look very smart," compliments Roger, looking at Joanna's light grey pleated skirt, open-collared white shirt with no tie, deep blue woollen jumper with gold-lined V-neck and cuffs, golden yellow tights and factory-polished black lace-up shoes. "You look like you mean business!"

"Herr Mozhoven says: *smart dress for smart learning*," informs Joanna, "actually, he says: *smart dress for smart playing,* but you know what I mean!"

"He's a very wise man," replies Roger, nodding in agreement.

"Now try your navy blue coat and golden yellow hat," requests Trish, helping Joanna insert one arm after the other and place the hat on her head, "they're both on the big side, but you'll grow into them!"

Joanna catches sight of herself in the mirror and likes what she sees. "Can I keep everything on for a bit?" she asks, adjusting the hat so she can see better.

"Just for a couple of hours," answers Roger. "You want to keep everything smart for your first day."

And with that, Joanna races upstairs to call Jenny.

"...and please, take your other clo..." says Trish, trailing off as she realises Joanna is nowhere to be seen, muttering under her breath, "...kids! When will they ever do anything before being asked?"

"...I like my hat!" says Joanna, revolving her head to show Jenny, who's staring back at her on the computer, "What do you think?"

"I can't believe you have to wear a hat, Joanna," replies Jenny, shaking her head, "I would refuse!"

"I think it looks very smart!" states Joanna, "and I love all the colours together."

"My Mum says your Mum rang her yesterday, to see if I wanted to come and stay for a weekend before we go back to school..." says Jenny, matter-of-factly, given how much she and Joanna have been talking about it since Joanna moved, "...come up on the train, and you'll pick me up from the station..."

"And...and?" excites Joanna, "What did your Mum say?"

"She said she'd think about it and let your Mum know!" replies Jenny, smiling and raising two sets of crossed fingers for Joanna to see.

"When will you know?" asks Joanna, "I'll get my Mum to chase!"

"I know my Mum!" replies Jenny, "She'll probably say I'm too young to travel alone and she's too busy to bring me...so don't get your hopes up!"

"I hope you can," says Joanna, raising *her* two sets of crossed fingers for Jenny to see, "then I can show you around. You can see my piano...and we can have midnight feasts in my playroom!"

Joanna and Jenny chat for twenty more minutes. They could talk longer, but Trish gives the signal she agreed with Joanna at breakfast: *Three buzzes on the KITCHEN servant bell means piano practice.* "Call you tomorrow, Jenny," says Joanna, waving goodbye. "Not sure if I'll be able to sleep tonight, thinking about what your Mum will say!"

Still dressed in her new uniform, Joanna makes her way to the living room and begins to practise - the piano book still open at the page from yesterday's lesson. She manages to get the first four bars sounding better before she begins to get bored and her mind starts to wander. She rubs her hands under the piano again and finds the two levers, rolling them between her fingers and thumbs - *little angel* and *little devil* suddenly appearing - each trying to help her decide what to do!

"Herr Mozhoven said: *don't open them both.*" debates Joanna with contributions from *little angel* followed by the ever-convincing *little devil*, "He actually said: *don't play them both together*, nothing about opening both, so where's the harm in just opening?"

Joanna pushes both levers and watches the clockwork mechanism slide both covers back to reveal the red and green keys. She walks down to the red key and plays it - once again experiencing the bassist, lowest, deepest, heaviest note. Then she walks down to the green key and plays it - once again experiencing the treble-ist, highest, shrillest, tightest note. She repeats this a few times - each time enjoying the experiences more and more!

These notes are so magical," Joanna says to herself - *little devil* drowning out *little angel*, "surely, playing both at the same time will double the experience!"

Whichever way she tries, Joanna can't reach both keys at the same time! She racks her brain and inspiration strikes. "The *seed dibbler* set from the greenhouse!"

Joanna runs up to the playroom and finds the box where she left, after showing Jenny - who, it must be said, was a little underwhelmed!

Rather than lugging the whole box set downstairs, Joanna takes the *Papa Bear* device and makes her way downstairs, grabbing some tape and a pair of socks.

Joanna stands in front of the piano and extends the telescopic arms, so the downward-pointing dibblers line up with the red and green keys. Not wanting to damage the keys, she places a sock over each dibbler and applies tape - tape that doesn't want to stick to the sock until she's used the best part of half a roll on each!

Sitting on the stool, Joanna lifts the seed-dibbler into position and without further thought, she plays both keys at the same time...

Initially, everything seems fine - the red key makes the bassist, lowest, deepest, heaviest note and the green key makes the treble-ist, highest, shrillest, tightest note. Then it happens! The contrasting sounds *smash* into each other, creating a noise louder than thunder and a flash of light, brighter than lightning. The piano fills with multicoloured sparks as if a lit firework has been deliberately thrown into its works. The keys begin playing by themselves, rippling up and down the piano - again and again and again, making a familiar increasing and decreasing sound, then randomly playing, making twisted and manic sounds, as if played in anger. Joanna drops the seed-dibbler to the floor and sits, helplessly. Watching wide-eyed and transfixed, eyes shutting - fearful and frightened. Then comes the crescendo - the finale - an explosion of sound. The piano inhales the biggest possible breath and exhales with all its might - *BOOM* - blowing Joanna away from the piano, making her travel backwards across the living room floor...making her travel back in time...

Time Travels...

Joanna opens her eyes. She's on a crowded London train station platform. Steam train smoke fills the air. Brown leather suitcase rests at her feet...number *1765* hangs around her neck on a piece of string like she's a parcel ready for posting. *Mickey Mouse* dangles from her left shoulder - a red leather gas mask with two large, silver-framed, circular eyes and cylindrical filter, originally blue, now painted green for easy identification. She is dressed in a school uniform, but not the blue and golden yellow uniform - instead, an all grey ensemble with a pale blue shirt, a charcoal grey coat and no hat!

"All aboard!" shouts the guard, blowing hard on his whistle, "All aboard!"

18

Listen for your number to be called!

Joanna picks up her suitcase - the suitcase she packed with her Mum. *Essentials* - a vest, a pair of knickers, a petticoat, two pairs of stockings, six handkerchiefs, a slip, a blouse and a cardigan. Some *extras* - Mackintosh, Wellington boots, a pair of shoes and plimsolls. In her *wash kit* - a comb, a toothbrush, a facecloth, a bar of soap and a towel. Finally, some *treats* - a packet of nuts, an apple and some boiled barley sweets!

The suitcase weighs the same, whichever way Joanna carries it - left hand, right hand or both hands - too heavy for a ten-year-old. She imagines for a moment, "Why can't they make suitcases with wheels on?" as she watches others struggling with the same scenario, "...perhaps with an extending handle, so you don't have to bend down to pick it up!"

It is Joanna's life, packed into a single suitcase - all the belongings she's allowed to take...belongings she and her Mum tearfully packed the night before, saying their *goodbyes,* neither knowing when they'll see each other again. Joanna had squeezed in her three favourite cuddly toys - three brown bears her Dad gave her before departing for war, saying, "Look after these bears with all your love, Joanna," he said gently, *bear hugging* and staring into her weeping eyes, "they represent our family - Papa Bear, Mama Bear and you, Baby Bear - a family that loves you and a family that will be reunited, very soon. I promise."

Very soon became weeks. Weeks became months and months became a year. Operation *Pied Piper* is reactivated as London is bombed - night, after night, after night. Children and teachers are evacuated to safer locations, and unknown host-families open their homes to frightened children - children facing futures as orphans...returning to homeless mothers...with or without their conscripted fathers.

"Let me help you, Joanna," offers Mr Moss-Hogan kindly. He is Joanna's teacher - an elderly gentleman who fought in the First World War, now too old for fighting...thankfully, as Joanna likes Mr Moss-Hogan.

"Thank you, Sir!" replies Joanna, looking at the overhead luggage rack as a bridge too far, before plonking herself down in the window seat and listening to the distinctive noise of congregated children, chattering.

Some children see evacuation as an adventure, exuding energy and high pranks. Some struggle and sit sobbing, red-eyed and sniffling. Most, including Joanna, are indifferent and sit quietly with no choice but to believe, living amongst peas and potatoes must be better than dying amongst bombs and barrages.

Joanna hears the final whistle from the platform conductor, before three train *toot-toots* the signal for departure. The train grunts and groans. Levers eventually lift and rotate. Metal screeches on metal.

The platform disappears, then the train disappears, briefly dipped in darkness as it travels through North London tunnels - made more ghostly by hundreds of voices, *woo-wooing!*

Then grey turns to green and gravel turns to grass. The countryside.

"Let's a have a sing-song!" suggests Mr Moss-Hogan, sensing sadness and recognising too many hours to fill, "What about *Run, Rabbit, Run?*"

The carriage erupts into song with accompanying hand gestures and spreads like wildfire - within minutes the whole train *Bang! Bang! Bang! Bangs!* And *gets by without its rabbit pie!*

"Sir, Sir!" shouts Ted Mitchell, one of Joanna's fellow evacuees, "What about *A Bicycle Made for Two?*"

"Good idea, Ted," replies Mr Moss-Hogan, taking the train down a different track, singing, *"Daisy, Daisy, give me your answer do..."*

Thirty minutes pass before initial enthusiasm is replaced with yawns and distraction. Another carriage tries to spark life into *The Laughing Policeman* but to no avail.

Some children snap out the cards and play rummy, showing off their shuffling skills and pretending to deal like casino croupiers!

There's no Wi-Fi, telephone network or in-seat entertainment...

Mr Moss-Hogan gathers a few children closer, including Joanna and offers to read a story. He lets the children choose between *Swallows and Amazons* and *The Secret Island* - two stories both involving children on an adventure. "*Swallows and Amazons,* it is, then!" he says, opening the book and quipping, "If you're sitting comfortably, then I'll begin...*Roger, aged seven, and no longer the youngest of the family, ran in wide zigzags, to and fro, across the steep field...*"

The train guard walks up the train, warning everyone of imminent arrival and final destination. There's an audible fluttering of tummy-filled butterflies. Everyone's scared, but given strength in numbers, no one knows if they'll be partnered or alone. Which host-family will be their lucky recipient? Whether as siblings, they'll even get to stay together?

The children are herded off the train and into designated buses like sheep being prepared for market. The buses are two-toned cream and red, simply decked out in diamond-checked, brown and red fabric seats - intermittently secured to the ceiling with polished hand supports. The bus driver does his best to inject some fun, but everyone's tired, hungry and longing for a familiar family face. Mr Moss-Hogan checks the numbers on his sheet against the numbers hanging around the necks of the eighteen children in his charge.

"1765!" calls Mr Moss-Hogan with no answer and beginning to show concern, "Where's 1765?"

"I'm here!" shouts Joanna from the front of the bus, seeing Mr Moss-Hogan immediately shutting his eyes, as if thanking some greater being, "Sorry, Sir! I needed the toilet...I'd been hanging on since London!"

The bus ambles its way - firstly, through well-signed and ordered roads surrounded by blacked-out buildings, hiding inner life from the enemy overhead...then through less-populated streets on the outskirts and...finally, driving along tree-edged, narrow unmarked roads with low-hanging branches sometimes scraping the top of the bus keeping the children awake. The light begins to fail as the sun says hello to the moon like changing shift workers maintaining a twenty-four-hour factory operation. The bus changes gear and turns into a village car park - generally deserted at this time of day - now populated with awaiting *carriages*.

Mr Moss-Hogan exits the bus first, shaking hands with the awaiting billeting officer. The children are escorted into the village hall and onto the stage - in front of the equally apprehensive village folk - *ogling* and scrutinising the children like farmers selecting a prize bull!

The children don't choose their family - the family chooses them.

After a little toing and froing, Mr Moss-Hogan finally reads out numbers and selected children are welcomed by their corresponding family.

Twelve children have been allocated - six remain. Joanna feels like one of the weaker football players, left at the end of selection for a *shirts* versus *skins* playground match - where both captains are trying *not* to select them!

"And that leaves you six!" says Mr Moss-Hogan, clutching his clipboard to his chest, "Three boys and three girls! You're with me. We're all staying at *Fortuna House* with Lady Fitzroy, but apparently, she's running a little late!"

"I'm so sorry!" bellows a confident woman's voice from the back of the hall as Lady Fitzroy bounds in with two accompanying teenage girls, "You must think us so rude!"

"No problem, Lady Fitzroy," replies Mr Moss-Hogan, introducing himself, then turning to Joanna and the other five children, "and these are your children!"

"It's a pleasure to meet you all," replies Lady Fitzroy, giving the children a much-needed smile before pointing, "please, take those wretched numbers from around your necks and introduce yourselves by name."

The children do as they're told, then nervously reply in turn, "Dillon. Joanna. Derek. David. June. Judy."

"Goodness me!" replies Lady Fitzroy, shaking each child by the hand, "What are the chances of having three handsome chaps with names all beginning with *D* and three gorgeous girls with names all beginning with *J*. How wonderful!" enthuses Lady Fitzroy, turning to Mr Moss-Hogan and nodding, "And these are my lovely daughters - Charlotte and Harriet...Charlie and Harrie! Now, let's get you all home, get you fed and get you settled in!"

19

We'll all get along if we all pull together!

"Good morning, Poppet!" says Lady Fitzroy, in a voice loud enough to compete with any cockerel. Dressed in dungarees and wearing a beautiful red silk scarf gift-wrapping her head, she continues, "Now you must be Joanna. Sit yourself down - I've made you *dippy egg and soldiers!*"

"Egg-cellent!" jokes Joanna nervously, as she sits down and smiles at the other children who have long-finished, their empty eggshells turned upside down to fake fullness!

"We didn't wake you, Joanna..." begins June, finishing her mouthful with a back-handed wipe across her mouth.

"...'cos you were away with the fairies!" finishes Judy, gulping a glass of water.

"I struggled to get to sleep," adds Joanna, nodding to Mr Moss-Hogan, then catching one of the boy's eyes and immediately turning away, "but then fell into a really deep sleep!"

Truth be told, Joanna pretended to be asleep, so she could get ready on her own - being an only child, she's not used to so much sharing and bathroom queuing!

Lady Fitzroy has put them all on the top floor, including Mr Moss-Hogan. The girls are sharing the front-left room, the boys are sharing the front-right room, and Mr Moss-Hogan is acting as dorm-master with his own room, back right. Each child has a metal bed, a reasonably comfy mattress, adequate bedlinen and a simple set of drawers for their belongings. The girls have one bathroom, and the boys have another - which Mr Moss-Hogan also uses, being a boy, too!

"There you go, Darling," says Lady Fitzroy, plonking a boiled egg and four soldiers in front of Joanna, "freshly laid this morning!"

"Thank you, Lady Fitzroy," replies Joanna, trying to think of the last time she had an egg - now a rationed commodity…along with bacon, meat, fish, butter, sugar, milk and cereals, to name but a few!

'Now that's enough of the formalities," says Lady Fitzroy, "just call me *Fitzy* - it's a nickname my husband gave me, and now everyone just calls me *Fitzy!*"

'Thank you…Fitzy." says Joanna, struggling with the informality. "Has your husband gone to war?"

'Yes. Lord Fitzroy and my son, Alfred - Charlie and Hattie's elder brother, are both fighting. Lord Fitzroy's a General in the Royal Engineers and Freddie's in the Royal Air Force…flying spitfires!"

Joanna dips a *soldier* into her egg. The yolk spills over, runs down the side of the egg and onto the plate, making Joanna stop and think for a moment, "Why does there have to be war? Why do people have to die? Why can't everyone get on? It doesn't make any sense!"

'Right, children, now that you're all fed and ready for the day, I thought I'd say a few things," says Fitzy, standing in front of the stove and beckoning Charlie and Harrie - also dressed in dungarees and heads gift-wrapped in silk scarves, to stand with her. "Firstly, this isn't holiday camp. Nor, might I hasten to add, is it a strict boarding school! However, we are living in tough times and as such, we all must adapt…fit in…pull our weight. All respect to the boys in the room, but *us* girls are having to do everything now - all the jobs our fathers, brothers and husbands normally did. Here at Fortuna House, we've been asked to turn our land into a smallholding and *dig for victory!*" says Fitzy, patriotically raising her mug of tea - also rationed. "The consolation is that we have access to more food like the eggs you've just eaten - normally rationed and considered a luxury. We have three smashing girls who help run the farm - our *land girls* - they live in the lodge at the end of *Longfield*. You'll meet them later. Actually,

I've just remembered...you're not going to believe it children, but they're sisters, and all have names beginning with *M!*"

"Mary, Mollie and Maud," adds Charlie with a reassuring smile from Fitzy.

"So, everyone here, will have daily tasks to carry out and about on the *farm*," continues Fitzy, highlighting *farm* with raised quote marks, "and when you're not doing these tasks or going to school with Mr Moss-Hogan, you'll be expected to assist in the kitchen - wash up, iron and help with general cleaning."

The children are shell-shocked. It all sounds like hard work.

"Now this may all sound like hard work," anticipates Fitzy, seeing the shock in the children's eyes, "but I assure you, once you've got the hang of your chores and if we all pull together, then it *will* become easier - I promise! In fact, there's no reason why it can't be fun, and we should all try to make it fun, yes! Oh...and did I forget to say? There will be treats along the way!"

The children breathe a sigh of relief. At least they've got each other - many evacuees don't have this.

"Charlie's in charge of the boys and Harrie's in charge of the girls," concludes Fitzy. "May I suggest that once we've all washed up, you put on your Wellington boots. B*oys* - you meet Charlie at the back door and *girls* - you meet Harrie at the front door. Mr Moss-Hogan - you meet me here, and I'll give you the tour!"

Joanna, June and Judy are waiting for Harrie by the front door, getting to know each other. Once they've established where each of them lives in London, how many brothers and sisters they have and whether their dads are in the army, navy or air force, the subject inevitably turns to boys!

"I think Dillon likes you, Joanna." says June, smiling and nodding, "He's always looking at you!"

"No, he's not!" replies Joanna, avoiding eye contact, kicking the gravel with her right foot and pretending she hasn't noticed, "...which one's Dillon?"

"You like him," adds Judy, "I can tell!"

"I like Derek," says June, "but I'm not sure if he likes me!"

"They're just stinky boys." declares Joanna, "Stinky boys who pick their noses and don't wash!"

The three girls burst into laughter.

"I'm glad you're all getting along so well," says Harrie as she steps out of the front door to join them, "follow me. We're off to the stables!

As they turn into the stableyard, the three girls are immediately hit with the overpowering odour of farmyard animals - the sick-making smell of fresh dung!

"That smells disgusting!" screams June, hiding her nose in her arm, "It's worse than the sewer works down the road at home!"

"You'll get used to it," remarks Harrie, laughing and shaking her head at their preciousness, "I don't know...*you, city girls!*"

"I suppose it's no worse than stinky boys," says Judy, cupping and releasing her nose - trying to acclimatise.

"I don't know what you're all going on about!" Joanna says in a muffled voice, wearing *Mickey Mouse* and peering at everyone through the misted glass, "We were issued these in case of gas!"

Everyone falls into fits of laughter - June and Judy wishing they'd brought their masks along too!

"You're like Huey, Dewey and Louie!" jokes Harrie - delighted she's looking after three giggling girls with a great sense of humour!

20

What's in a name!

"Hey, look in here!" squeals June, running over to the first stable, standing on tiptoes and staring in, "There are pigs!"

"And pigs here too!" squeaks Judy, running to the second stable, also standing on tiptoes and staring in, "One, two, three...six piglets and their Mum!"

Not to be outdone, Joanna runs to the third stable, expecting to find yet more pigs, but instead finding, "A cow!" she moos, "A black and white cow!"

Like a leapfrog, June leaves her pigs, peers in to see Judy's pigs, peeks into see Joanna's cow and then runs to the fourth stable - again standing on tiptoes and staring in to find, "A cow!" she moos, too, "A brown cow!"

By this time, Judy and Joanna have caught up and peer into see June's brown cow, all shouting, "How, now, brown cow!"

Harrie stands and watches, reminding herself how special it must be, seeing something for the first time - something you've only ever read about or seen in pictures.

Joanna, June and Judy run to the other side - all three standing on tiptoes and staring in to see an empty stable...empty of animals, but full of equipment - large vats, turning things, buckets, yolks and much, much more. Slightly disappointed, they run to the next stable, immediately stepping back as a colossal shire horse pokes out his head and gives a lip-rippling *neigh* as if to say, "Hey, hello, I'm hungry!"

"He's like the horse that delivers the beer at home!" shouts Judy, edging closer to offer her hand in friendship.

"*He*...is a girl!" shouts Harrie, "The boy is next door!"

And sure enough, another huge shire horse head appears.

"They're ginormous!" shouts Joanna, never having stood so close to one before, "They hardly fit through the door!"

"Mumsy bought them a few days ago," informs Harrie, walking over to join the girls, "to pull carts and plough fields."

"And what's in the last stable?" enquires Joanna, running over to peer inside, "...more equipment?"

"No, that's Jenny!" replies Harrie, joining Joanna to peer in, "A donkey! She's been part of the family for years and helps out at school fetes, the annual nativity play and pulls a small trap around the grounds."

"She's beautiful," replies Joanna, pulling herself onto the half stable door, making kissing sounds and clapping her hands to beckon Jenny over, "I never knew donkeys could come in snow-white!"

June and Judy peer in, too, but they're more interested in returning to the pigs.

"We thought it would be nice if you girls named the animals...other than Jenny of course," says Harrie, pulling a small pencil and notepad from her back pocket. "They're all new here, and we knew you were coming, so we held off!

The girls throw ideas into the hat, making their opinions heard - sometimes quite vociferously! *"You can't call an animal that!"* or *"That's more of a dog's name!"* Until finally, they agree.

"So, we're agreed," confirms Harrie, reading her notebook, after pages of crossed out attempts, "we're going with the flower theme. The cows are called *Dandelion* and *Daisy*. The pigs are called *Petunia* and *Primrose*, and the shire horses are called *Foxglove* and *Hollyhock!*"

"Hurray!" shout the girls, nodding at each other - pleased with their choices.

"So, who wants to paint new nameplates?" asks Harrie, going to the equipment stable and returning with a small pot of bottle green paint and a small pot of gold paint.

"Oooh, me, me!" the girls shout, putting their hands up as high as they can, hoping the highest will be chosen, "Please, Harrie, me!"

"I think you should all do it," says Harrie, thinking it best to keep the peace. "June and Judy, you can paint the nameplates bottle green and Joanna, you can paint the names in gold!"

When the bottle green paint is dry, Joanna uses a milking stool to stand on and tries her hardest to paint the names as smartly as possible. The problem is, some names are longer than others...she misjudges and ends up having to squeeze some of the letters in at the end!

Harrie hands a pitchfork to each girl and assigns a stable to muck out

"Can we do it all together?" asks Judy, "It'll be quicker and more fun...and that *is* what Fitzy said - for us to have fun!"

"Very well!" replies Harrie, realising *three against one* isn't a fair match, "As long as you work together, there are no slackers, and there isn't too much *mucking* around!"

Joanna, June and Judy - now immune to the smell...almost! Muck out the dirty straw. Harrie pulls a small cart of fresh straw and tops up the bedding, fills water troughs and adds the feed.

"I'm impressed!" compliments Harrie, "You've taken to it like ducks to water!"

"You did say we were like Huey, Dewey and Louie!" jests Joanna.

"And I am right!" replies Judy, "Working together *is* more efficient and more fun than individually!"

"Yes, you're right," concedes Harrie, giving a nod of surrender, "many hands do make light work!"

"So, are we finished after this?" enquires June, desperate to hear *yes!*

"Not quite," replies Harrie, "then I'll show you your daily task!"

"You mean *this* isn't our daily task?" replies Judy, deflated.

"Mucking out the stables is like cleaning your teeth and making your bed," replies Harrie, "We all have to do it, and it's not considered a task!"

"So, what is our task?" asks Joanna, now intrigued.

"There are three tasks you can make a rota for," informs Harrie, before looking at Judy with a wry smile, "unless, of course, you want to stick to doing one thing!"

"Depends what the tasks are," replies Judy, duplicating a wry smile.

"Milking, butter churning and egg collecting," announces Harrie, waiting for negative responses, only to see the girls' faces light up.

"We get to milk a cow?" amazes Joanna, "...milk a real-life cow!"

"And make butter?" replies June, confused, "What from?"

"Cow's milk, of course!" responds Judy, "Where did you think butter came from?"

Joanna, June and Judy follow Harrie over to the equipment stable and get a lesson in butter churning and cheesemaking. Although, the girls won't be making cheese - that's down to Charlie and Harrie...they see how it starts from milk and involves separating the curds and whey!

Then the girls go over to Dandelion, for a lesson in milking.

"It's always best to speak nicely to Dandelion and Daisy," begins Harrie. "You are, after all, going to become best of friends!"

"Will they kick?" asks June, frightened at standing so close to a real cow!

"They may stamp their feet if they're in a bad mood!" replies Harrie.

"Don't we all?" jokes Judy, also intimidated by the thought of milking a real cow!

"So that's why we sit to the side," continues Harrie, "on a special three-legged milking stool."

"Three legs make it stable," adds Joanna, "however uneven the ground is."

"Very good, Joanna," replies Harrie, impressed with Joanna's knowledge, continuing, "then you grab a teat between your thumb and forefinger like so...and pull-down and to the side like so...and then the milk flows like so!"

The sound of milk, squirting into a metal bucket, rings around the stable, resulting in swapped glances of excitement!

Joanna, June and Judy take turns. It's more difficult than it looks. Joanna gets the hang of it quickest - Judy second, through gritted determination - eventually June, who starts off too timidly, before pulling harder...spurred on by Harrie's encouragement, "Don't worry, June, it won't hurt Dandelion!"

Suddenly a faint *chugging* noise can be heard. It gets louder and louder. The girls look at each other, hoping that one of them will have the answer, but no such luck.

"That'll be *Bessie!*" adds Harrie, mischievously as the *chugging* becomes more distinctive and loud.

Then into the stableyard drive Mary, Mollie and Maud - on *Bessie*, the trailer-pulling tractor...full of hay bales!

21

A midnight swim with geese!

Mary keeps the engine ticking over, while Mollie and Maud jump down from the trailer to open the barn doors - directing Mary as she circles around and reverses into the barn, turns off the tractor and jumps down to join her sisters.

"Morning Mary, morning Mollie, morning Maud!" shouts Harrie as she walks over and gives each girl a hug and a kiss of greeting on the cheek, "I see you've been busy!"

"We started at the crack of dawn," replies Mary, wiping the sweat from her brow with a sacrificial sleeve, before rolling up both shirt sleeves.

"Even before the cockerel crowed!" adds Mollie, putting both hands in her dungarees pockets and sighing deeply.

"Well, you know what they say," poses Maud, sipping from a leather-clad water flask before passing it to Mary, "you have to make hay while the sun shines!"

"These must be the three scallywags from the city!" jokes Mary, turning to see Joanna, June and Judy standing at Dandelion's door - shy and overawed by the three, larger than life, *land girls!*

"Get yourselves over here!" beckons Harrie, open-armed, introducing them to Mary, Mollie and Maud, "This is Joanna, this is June, and this is Judy - my three very helpful, *helping hands!"*

If Joanna had to guess, she'd say Mary was 25. Mollie was 22 and Maud was 19 - three naturally beautiful girls, beaming and flourishing in the fresh air. If they had any resentment to working the land, they didn't show it. They know if they'd been born boys, they'd be off fighting, brandishing a rifle instead of a rake. They're playing their part for the country, and blistered hands are a small price to pay!

"Good to have you on board," says Mollie, shaking Joanna, Judy and June's hands. "The more girls, the merrier!"

"Yep," adds Maud, "*us* girls, gotta stick together - like birds of a feather!"

"Enough of the introductions," says Mary, joking, but appearing slightly curt, "we've got work to do - these hay bales aren't going to unload themselves!"

"And I'm going to show the girls how to collect eggs," says Harrie, looking at Joanna, June and Judy, as she rubs her hands together, jesting, "let's see who's chicken!"

"Don't listen to her, girls!" shouts Maud, thrusting a pitchfork into a hay bale, "Sometimes you gotta break a few eggs to make an omelette!"

Joanna makes a mental note - Maud has all *the sayings*, Mollie's *the gentle one*, and Mary's *the boss!*

Harrie grabs a wicker basket and unlocks the chicken-wired door to the left section of the barn, ushering in Joanna, June and Judy before any chickens can escape. There in front of them is the most luxurious chicken coop they could ever imagine - a Victorian horse carriage! Chickens clamber up purposefully-made wooden planks, through the carriage and out the other side - some nesting inside the carriage, some nesting on free-standing platforms. A couple of cockerels are perched higher up, occasionally crowing.

"Brac...brac, brac, brac!" begins Judy, mimicking a chicken as she flaps her wing-shaped arms, sticks out her bottom and moves her head in and out. "I'm a chicken, Harrie!"

Unfortunately, she looks more like a dog trying to vomit than a chicken walking!

"You have to tread very carefully!" informs Harrie, "You can find eggs anywhere!"

"Like here!" says Judy, stopping in her tracks and lifting her leg to reveal a smashed egg - yolk dripping from the sole of her shoe, "Sorry, Harrie."

"Eggs-actly!" replies Harrie, "It's no *yolking* matter! Let that be a lesson to you all! I've already been here this morning to get your breakfast eggs, but let's see if we can find a few more."

"Here's one!" shouts Joanna, searching the barn like an Easter hunt and carefully placing the egg in the straw-lined basket, "And here's another!"

After they've exhausted the egg supply, Harrie and the land girls take Joanna, Judy and June back to the house for lunch. Charlie and the boys are already tucking into bowls of vegetable soup, as they sit and all swap stories on the morning's activities.

Fitzy loves the camaraderie. Joanna sees her give Mr Moss-Hogan the thumbs up, who reciprocates immediately.

The afternoon is equally action-packed - less with chores, more with the land girls taking Charlie and the boys and Harrie and the girls on the trailer, pulling them with Bessie around the grounds, showing them all the nooks and crannies. They see what's being grown in the land and they pass the hunting lodge, where the land girls are staying.

After tea and freshly baked scones at four o'clock, Charlie finds an old cricket bat, a *seen-better-days* tennis ball and everyone plays French cricket on the lawn, in front of the lake. It's followed by *kick the can* and a gentle *tag* version of *British Bulldog!*

Joanna can't believe it's only been twenty-four hours since London - twenty-four hours since a different world. She knows she'll miss home, but she's enjoying herself, and that feels good - long may it last!

"Suppertime!" bellows Fitzy from the back door, "Come and get it before it gets cold...and remember to wash your hands!"

Although the diet's basic, it's wholesome and filling, and Joanna never hears anyone complain - everyone eats what they're given and they're thankful for it.

Supper is followed by bath time, a story from Mr Moss-Hogan and then forty-five minutes listening to the radio. Joanna studies the radio's cathedral-like appearance of gothic arches and intricate details - deliberately grand, in recognition of its significance within the home. It is the focal point. Everyone sits around it and stares at it, even though it's motionless and only makes sound! It is the window to the outside world for communication, entertainment, information and news - good, bad and indifferent...its single *speaker*, spreading hope and unity.

Then, bed.

Charlie briefs the boys and Harrie briefs the girls, agreeing a wake-up time and who's doing what - Joanna's milking Daisy, Judy's milking Dandelion and June's collecting eggs...followed by all three, mucking out and butter churning.

"Night, girls," says Mr Moss-Hogan, after Harrie departs downstairs, "lights out!"

A few hours later...

"Psst! Psst!" hisses someone, hidden by darkness, "Joanna, wake-up! It's me, Harrie!"

"Is it morning?" replies Joanna, unsure if she's coming or going or whether it's just a dream.

"No, it's midnight," replies Harrie, "grab your towel and a pair of knickers - we're going for a midnight swim!"

Joanna stretches and sees Judy and June suffering the same sequence. They tiptoe out of their room to find Charlie with the boys...

Thirty-six steps later, they reach the ground floor - boys and girls giggling, trying hard not to make a noise, but failing miserably!

Then they're out of the back door and onto the lawn - running down to the lake and led by Harrie and Charlie...two moonlit silhouettes, and this is not their first time!

The sky is charcoal blue with lighter coloured clouds, partly blocking the moon, passing - to be replaced by another a minute or so later.

Pyjamas are thrown to the floor as everyone prepares for, *"Aww, it's freezing!"* and, *"Goodness me, it's cold enough to make your heart stop!"*

"Joanna!" whispers June.

"What's up?" replies Joanna, eager to join the others.

"I can't swim," says June, "I was going to start lessons, then the war started!"

"Harrie says it's not that deep," replies Joanna, grabbing June's hand. "We'll jump in together!"

Fun and frivolity are rudely interrupted by whirring noises in the sky. Everyone stops splashing and stands still - stargazing. The whirring gets louder and louder. Then three enemy *black shadow* bombers, fly overhead like migrating geese - retreating after dropping disaster on armament factories and steel mills. They're so low, David and Derek later claim they can see men's faces staring down. It's a harsh reminder that war is everywhere, even here!

The children quietly gather their clothes and go back to bed - not a word is spoken ...everything has already been said.

22

Encore! Encore!

"Now a little birdie tells me…Mr Moss-Hogan is an excellent piano player," begins Fitzy, grabbing her mug of tea and sitting down at the breakfast table - mentioning nothing about last night's swim and serving dippy eggs and soldiers, just like the day before.

"You flatter me," replies Mr Moss-Hogan, turning two-tones deeper red and laughing nervously, "I'd say more of an average piano player!"

"You're right, Fitzy," adds Joanna, keen to endorse Mr Moss-Hogan, "Sir has played for some very important people…he's even played for the King's mother-in-law!"

"I think we can drop the formalities while we're not at school, Joanna," says Mr Moss-Hogan, taking a leaf out of Fitzy's book, "Please, call me William."

"If Mr Moss-Hogan…William…is up for it," continues Fitzy, "then I'd like to suggest a welcoming party this evening! A few nibbles and drinks - obviously lemonade for you children…accompanied by a small piano recital from William. My husband is an excellent pianist and would have been the first to volunteer, but sadly, he's not here. We have an exquisite piano, dying to be played. So, what do you say, William?"

"WILLIAM! WILLIAM! WILLIAM!" chant the children, banging their cutlery on the table.

"Alright, alright!" surrenders William, smiling - realising he has little choice, "I'll play!"

"HURRAY!" shout the children, delighted their contribution sways his decision!

"That's settled then," says Fitzy, giving William a smile to show her gratitude, "Six-thirty in the living room…we'll invite the land girls and children. It will be a treat, so *you* just turn up and enjoy yourselves!"

Joanna, Judy and June return to the stableyard after breakfast following a six o'clock early start to milk Dandelion and Daisy and collect freshly laid eggs. They grab a pitchfork and begin raking dirty straw like it's second nature - Harrie, occasionally making an appearance for quality control.

"The smell isn't so bad, today!" remarks Judy, sniffing the air like a dog in search of a scent.

"I quite like it now!" admits June, realising this will spark ridicule

"I'm not surprised, June," jokes Joanna, "You like stinky boys!"

"So, what do we think the story is with William?" poses Judy, relieving June of any further leg-pulling, "Do we think he's married?"

"He's definitely *been* married," responds Joanna. "He wears a wedding ring...but I'm not sure what's happened to his wife."

"Perhaps she passed away," suggests June, "or stayed in London to help there."

"Or perhaps she's a spy!" adds Judy, letting her imagination run wild. "Who'd suspect an older woman to go undercover, making friends with the enemy to find out top secrets?"

"I think I'd like to be a spy!" says Joanna, "I think women would make excellent spies..."

"Have you finished girls?" interrupts Harrie, peering into Jenny's stable, "The butter's not going to churn itself!"

Joanna, June and Judy follow Harrie over to the equipment stable for butter churning. The cream of the milk has been sitting in the butter churn for a few hours and is ripe and ready. Each girl, including Harrie, has a clear glass butter churn, complete with metal turning-device and begins rotating the handle to operate the churners - gliding effortlessly through the liquid milk like a hot knife through butter!

"Are we done yet?" asks Judy after ten minutes - all the girls complaining of sore arms!

"About thirty minutes more!" replies Harrie, sympathetic to their moaning…her arms are also tiring and hurting.

"Thirty minutes!" exclaims June, "That's torture!"

"Are we done yet?" Judy asks again after forty minutes, having asked every five minutes as a running joke.

As the milk turns to butter and arms become exhausted, churning becomes harder and harder and slower and slower - almost grinding to a halt.

"I think we're ready to strain the buttermilk," announces Harrie, looking to rally enthusiasm, "then pat the butter!"

"I knew a dog called *Pat*," adds Joanna, "*Pat* the dog!" she jokes - audible groans churning around the stable, "Perhaps he's friends with *Pat* the butter!"

Each girl strains their buttermilk into a big blue and white striped ceramic jug, ready to make pancakes for afternoon tea - places the remaining butter onto a wooden board and with wooden butter pats, pats the butter into a rectangular shape or a shape best resembling a rectangle, finally inscribing their names like an artist, signing a work of art.

"Well done, girls!" applauds Harrie, "Your very first butter pats. Let's get them into the larder before they go off!"

All the children have an early supper and bath around six, so they're ready for the evening party.

Fitzy has tied red white and blue bunting around the walls. Charlie has hand-painted '*WELCOME TO OUR NEW FRIENDS!*' in big black letters on a makeshift banner, also splattered with red hearts. Harrie has made the tastiest, freshest, most lemony and

...most moreish real lemonade? The children can't get enough of it, refilling large ladles-full, from the gargantuan glass bowl, until it's nearly gone in ten minutes.

Fitzy chinks her glass with a metal spoon to get everyone's attention. "I'd like to say a few words before our beloved new friend - William, entertains us with a little tinkling on the piano!" toasts Fitzy, staring around the room to acknowledge everyone. "These unfortunate and distressing circumstances may have brought us together, but friendship finds itself through thick and thin. I welcome you all, and assure you - we'll face this absurd adversity together and get through it...as one!" concludes Fitzy raising her glass with everyone following suit...some with empty glasses, namely, Joanna, Judy and Dillon!

"To us all!"

"To us all!" repeats everyone, as they take a seat on a wooden chair - the type found in a school or a church, brought down from the storage room for the occasion.

William stands at the piano and makes a small introduction.

"Firstly, on behalf of the children, I'd like to thank Fitzy, Charlie and Harrie for putting on such a wonderful spread," he begins - all the children clapping and stomping their feet in agreement. "Secondly, I'd like to say what a privilege it is, to have the chance to play on this amazing, *one-of-a-kind* piano; the *Bösendorfer 90* - so-called because it has two extra keys! So, with this in mind, I have selected two pieces, written especially for this *very* piano - one using the *extra* bass note and the other using the *extra* treble note. Thank you."

William pushes the left lever on the underside of the piano to reveal the red-enamelled, *extra* bass key. He places the first music sheet on the stand and begins playing - eyes closed, opening to turn the page when necessary and flicking his fringe to match the intensity of the music. Halfway through the piece...

he reaches over and plays the *red* key - everyone hears the bassist, lowest, deepest, heaviest note they've ever heard!

Then William pushes the right lever on the underside of the piano to reveal the green-enamelled, *extra* treble key - automatically concealing the extra bass key. He places the second music sheet on the stand and begins playing - again, eyes closed - again, opening to turn the page when necessary and again, flicking his fringe to match the intensity of the music. Towards the end of the piece, he reaches over and plays the *green* key - everyone hears the treble-ist, highest, shrillest, tightest note, ring out!

There is stunned silence when William finishes - even Fitzy is unaware of the piano's hidden feature.

"Bravo!" cries Fitzy, echoed by everyone, "Encore! Encore!"

"Thank you, thank you!" replies William, bowing three times and milking the applause, "perhaps I can play one more. This is a tune I've been working on recently - a tune inspired by wonderful women like you!" he says, making a small clapping gesture and looking at Fitzy, her daughters, the land girls and of course, Joanna, June and Judy, "A work in progress, entitled: *Women - we salute you!*"

As William plays the first few bars, Joanna feels a strange sensation - her eyes roll back and begin twirling inside her head, as if exploring her mind and entering a spiralling tunnel of flashing lights and multicolours, making her travel forwards in space...making her travel forwards in time!

Time travels...

She opens her eyes to find she's sitting at the piano in her living room, dressed in her blue and golden yellow uniform - seed-dibbler, resting at her feet...red and green keys both on show...

She's back to the present.

23

On your marks, get set...BAKE!

Joanna pulls the levers to conceal the extra keys, places the seed-dibbler under the sofa, away from view and continues to practise *Women: we salute you*. It now feels like the most familiar tune in the world as her fingers move from note to note, bar to bar and line to line until she finishes. The tune maybe short and sweet, but for Joanna, it's special - her first completed tune - a tune with meaning and memories. She turns around, expecting to see June and Judy or Fitzy and the girls or William, Mr Moss Hogan, but no one's there - she's alone. She looks again at the music for a name, only to discover that the writer is *anonymous!*

Joanna realises then, that her recollection is one way and that no memories of the present travel with her - perhaps just as well, considering the enormity of change and the complexity of dealing with such a comparison. She thinks it's best not to tell her parents - she doesn't want to risk the piano being fixed or lessons to cease with Herr Mozhoven. What Trish and Roger don't know, won't worry them!

Joanna has a sudden urge to bake!

"Mummy, I'm going to bake muffins!" declares Joanna, skipping into the kitchen and finding an apron - her favourite one...bright red and printed with *World's Best Baker & World's Best Mess Maker* in white swirly letters.

"You mean, you're going to turn the kitchen into a war zone," replies Trish, "exploding powder, utter chaos and leaving me with complete carnage to clean up!"

"I'll clean up!" announces Joanna, laying out her ingredients, "It's only fair for me to help and pull my weight!"

"I can't complain at that," replies Trish, taken aback, "but please, make sure you follow a recipe…experimental cooking might be fun, but when the results are inedible and end up in the bin, it makes it feel doubly expensive."

"I will, Mummy," replies Joanna, turning her birthday cookbook to the right page and placing it behind a plastic holder, "I'm going to make banana and toffee muffins…"

"Sounds scrumptious," says Roger, walking into the kitchen and putting the kettle on the stove, "perfect with my afternoon tea!"

"Did you know, they didn't have bananas in the Second World War?" states Joanna, measuring the correct flour dosage, adding, "…and eggs and sugar were rationed, along with milk and butter and chocolate and bacon."

"That's right," replies Roger, chucking a teabag into his cup, "the first time Grandma was given a banana, she bit into the skin like an apple!"

"And people used to give sugar and eggs as presents!" adds Trish, gesturing to Roger for a cup of coffee, "Grandpa Jo asked for sugar for his tenth birthday, so his Mum - your Great Nan, could make him a birthday cake!"

"You're joking!" replies Joanna, measuring 100 grams of sugar and cracking two eggs, "But Grandpa Jo was ten *after* the war!"

"Rationing went on until the mid-1950s," informs Roger, adding milk to the tea and coffee, "perhaps they should ration sugar again…what with all the problems of obesity and diabetes!"

"And did you know, they didn't have fridges in the Second World War," says Joanna, whisking her muffin mix - occasionally licking, making sure it *tastes right*, "or power showers…just baths!"

"Where's all this knowledge coming from?" asks Trish, grabbing a piece of cut banana…much to Joanna's annoyance…

"What did our relatives do in the war?" asks Joanna, ignoring Trish's question as she spoons muffin mix into bright yellow fluted paper holders, before placing them in the oven with Roger's helping hands.

"Your Great Papa - Grandpa Jo's Dad, was a Sergeant and was decorated for bravery during D-Day," replies Trish. "Grandpa Jo didn't see his Dad for six years and thought he was a stranger when he finally returned and knocked on the door."

"And your Great Grandad - Grandma's Dad, was in the medical corps," adds Roger, "attending to the wounded throughout Europe and Northern Africa, and was eventually sent to liberate concentration camps, unaware they were being sent to unearth unmentionable atrocities…"

"There are no winners in war…" adds Trish, shaking her head and sipping her coffee, "…it affects people their whole lives."

"And what about the women in our family?" asks Joanna, opening the oven to check on the muffins, "What did they do?"

"Great Grandma and her two sisters were *land girls!*" replies Roger, salivating at the sight of the nearly ready muffins, "Helping out on the farms."

"Your Great Nan, Grandpa Jo's Mum, was a spy!" adds Trish "…and apparently, very good at it!"

"Land girls and a spy, you say!" replies Joanna, "Unbelievably brilliant!"

"You should ask your grandparents, next time they come," says Roger, licking the mixer fork like a ten-year-old kid, "they'd love to tell you all about it, and they know all the details."

Joanna rests the muffins after taking them out of the oven. Once cooled, she covers them in toffee sauce and tops with a couple of banana slices. Joanna wishes she could call in June and Judy and

Charlie and Harrie from their chores and offer them a taste of *sweet* luxury - she can't wait to travel back in time to see them again!

Trish reminds Joanna that five o'clock is only ten minutes away. Joanna finishes clearing up, mainly with Trish's *helping hands* and runs up to change into a green satin dress for Herr Mozhoven!

"Sehr gut!" says Herr Mozhoven as Joanna finishes playing *Women: we salute you*, "Sehr gut, Yoanna! Und you have learnt this in ein very short time!"

"Thank you, Herr Mozhoven," replies Joanna, extremely pleased with herself.

"Right, please turn to page ten," requests Herr Mozhoven, "und you will learn a slightly more difficult und more moving tune: *Poppy: remember me!*"

"Is this another tune from the Second World War?" asks Joanna, turning to page ten and securing the pages.

"The First World War," replies Herr Mozhoven, "when millions of soldiers on both sides were killed on the battlegrounds of East und Western fronts. The poppy represents this bloodshed und acts as ein permanent symbol to never forget this ultimate sacrifice."

Joanna begins. The notes are more advanced, and the rhythm is more swaying and continuous. She imagines a red poppy in a muddy field, moving in the wind - weeping and mourning.

Joanna steps her way through the tune, struggling to press the notes with enough force to make a sound - Herr Mozhoven making it look and sound so easy!

"Please, practise this tune, Yoanna," concludes Herr Mozhoven as he dismantles his chair and replaces it in his inside jacket pocket, "und I will see you tomorrow."

Joanna runs upstairs to call Jenny. There's so much she wants to tell her, but is unsure how to even begin - will Jenny think her a dreamer or that she is someone who's completely lost the plot?

She rings and rings. There's no answer. She rings again and then again. "Jenny must be out," she says to herself as she makes her way downstairs, "perhaps I'll go and see June and Judy instead. I know it's naughty playing the extra piano keys, but no harm's done...and I did come back!"

Sitting on the stool, Joanna lifts the seed-dibbler into position and without further thought, plays both keys at the same time...

Just as before, the red key makes the bassist, lowest, deepest, heaviest note and the green key makes the treble-ist, highest, shrillest, tightest note. Then fireworks, thunder and lightning and manic piano playing! Joanna closes her eyes for the crescendo - *BOOM* - blowing her away from the piano...making her travel backwards across the living room floor...making her travel back in time...

Time travels...

Joanna opens her eyes. She's not on a train or in Fortuna House - she's in a small bedroom...one girl shaking her shoulders and another tickling her feet!

24

His master's voice!

"Wake up, Joanna, wake up!" shout Joanna's sisters - Jane and Jean, "It's Saturday! Master Robert's coming home from the war today, and we need to help Dad with the horses!"

Joanna reluctantly opens her eyes, but the thought of seeing Master Robert again, injects life and she springs out of bed to join the others in the bathroom. They fill a large bowl with jug-poured water and splash their faces to wake up and clean at the same time.

Joanna stares at her sisters - Jane is the eldest at sixteen, and Jean is in between, at thirteen. Dressed in brown knee-length dresses with white pinafores, they help each other tie their long brown hair with large bows - Joanna's bow is blue, Jane's bow is red, and Jean's bow is green...before carefully lacing and tying their black leather boots.

"Hurry up, girls!" hollers Hester - their Mother, standing at the bottom of the stairs and putting on her coat, "Come and get some breakfast - there's some porridge on the stove. I need to get to the house to help her Ladyship with preparation for Master Robert's return."

"Don't worry, Mother," replies Jane as they breeze past and enter the kitchen, "We can help ourselves. You hurry along. We'll get ourselves over to the stables as soon as we can."

"And remember!" adds Hester as she grabs her hat and opens the door, "Children are expected to be seen and not heard - especially when you're around her Ladyship."

Joanna's Mother is head-housekeeper at Fortuna House and Joanna's Father - Jim, is head-horseman...responsible for managing the stables, although, since horse conscription and his Lordship's love of the motorcar, Jim has become both horse and car mechanic!

Lord and Lady Buttontrop, kindly let Jim and Hester live in the old hunting lodge, located at the end of *Longfield*, which Joanna, Jane and Jean, now call home. It may be small, but what it lacks in size it more than makes up for in character and warmth.

After a wholesome bowl of porridge, the girls make their way over to the stables. As they approach the lake to the rear of Fortuna House, they're met with loads of licking and tail wagging - Ludwig.

"Get down, Ludwig!" shouts Joanna, wrestling and cuddling him at the same time, "I need to keep my dress clean!"

Ludwig is the same age as Joanna, but in dog years, he's about 70! Lord and Lady Buttontrop bought him for Master Robert on his tenth birthday - a strong black working Labrador with an amazing shiny silk coat, gifted with endless energy and superb retrieving skills. Master Robert called him *Ludwig* after his passion for the piano and enthusiastic love of Beethoven. Joanna, Jane and Jean consider Ludwig to be as much their dog as Master Robert's - especially Joanna, who seems to have an extra-special bond.

"It's almost like he knows," says Joanna, stroking Ludwig's tummy like he's a big baby, "You know Master Robert's coming home today...don't you, Ludwig?"

Joanna, Jane, Jean and Ludwig continue to the stables. The eight stables used to house thoroughbred hunting and driving horses now two ageing mares reside, Emmeline and Millicent, named as

Before the war, Lady Buttontrop had been a keen supporter of *The Suffragist* movement - spearheaded by Millicent Fawcett, to improve the role of middle-class women in society and win them the right to vote. Support for *The Suffragettes overtook this* - this time, spearheaded by Emmeline Pankhurst, now focused on the plights of working-class women and securing the vote for all women. Emmeline advocated extreme measures, whereas Millicent's were more peaceful. Lady Buttontrop wavered between the two - spurred on and appalled by unfair working conditions and lack of influence for change. As a sign of respect for King and Country, activities are placed on hold during the war, but defiantly, Lady Buttontrop names the horses *Emmeline and Millicent*, to act as a reminder.

Jim has the sizeable black carriage out in the yard - gleaming and resplendent. He grooms the horses but has asked Joanna, Jane and Jean to come and braid the horses' manes - as much as he tries, he can never do it quite as well as them.

"Hi, girls," greets Jim, stopping to admire his three beautiful daughters, "the ribbons are in the barn, and I'll fetch the stools for you to stand on."

An hour later, Emmeline and Millicent look magnificent. Jim attaches them to the carriage and awaits his Lordship. Meanwhile, Joanna, Jane and Jean, take turns sitting high up alongside Jim in the driving seat.

"Quickly, girls!" hurries Jim, giving each girl a chance to hold the driving whip and feel the reins, "His lordship said he'd be here for nine o'clock. Master Robert's train arrives at ten o'clock, and he wants to be at the station, ready and waiting."

"Stand and deliver!" shouts Joanna, imagining Dick Turpin approaching, "Your money or your life!"

True to his word, Lord Buttontrop arrives at the stables at nine o'clock.

"Morning, Jim," booms Lord Buttontrop, smiling at Joanna, Jane and Jean, as they stand back and curtsy, "and good morning to you three! What a lovely morning for Master Robert's return. Please, say you'll hang around, girls, to say hello to him."

"The girls would love to," replies Jim, on their behalf, watching them nod in agreement and excitement - Master Robert is as much their friend as the only child of Lord and Lady Buttontrop.

"Actually, Jim," continues Lord Buttontrop, "seeing as it's such a fine morning, I think I'll take the motorcar!"

"Very good, your Lordship," replies Jim, seeing the disappointment in the girls' faces - their expert braiding going to waste, "let me get it for you."

"Please, don't worry yourself," replies Lord Buttontrop, "I can get it."

Two minutes later, there's a cranking noise, followed by the roar of an engine and pedal-to-the-floor revving! Jim calms the horses - they haven't got used to their mechanical counterpart. Then a brown-leather-goggled Lord Buttontrop, appears from the barn in a gorgeous, open-topped silver car with bright red leather seats, grinding through the gears and gesturing *goodbye* as he steers erratically past - through the stable exit and beyond. "*Honk, honk!*"

"I do hope he gets there in one piece," remarks Jim, smiling at the girls, "...and without knocking anything over!"

Joanna, Jane and Jean decide to stand halfway up the drive to greet Master Robert. Lady Buttontrop positions herself at the front door with Hester and Jim to her side - on hand to make sure everything's perfect for her son's return.

The girls can hear the distinctive motorcar roar, getting ever-louder, until Lord Buttontrop sweeps in through the pillared-gate and onto the drive. Joanna, Jane and Jean wave frantically and shout greetings, as the car drives past. They try to run alongside but quickly fall behind, arriving out of breath, as Lord Buttontrop gets out of the car - his face, serious and forlorn.

Joanna, Jane and Jean stand still and silent - unsure of what to say or how to react.

Initial exuberance is replaced with respectful silence. Lord Buttontrop circles his motorcar to open the door for Master Robert.

Master Robert - decorated and dressed in a khaki-coloured Captain's uniform. Master Robert - eyes heavily bandaged...blinded by gas, just one week prior. Master Robert - clambering to stand...aided by a stick, his father now his crutch.

"Robert, darling!" welcomes Lady Buttontrop, attempting to disguise her shock and concern, "Welcome home."

"Hello, Mother!" replies Master Robert, *looking* in her general direction, "It's good to be home!"

Lord Buttontrop slams the car door, to witness his son wince and cower with fright. Master Robert can't see the shock, sadness and sympathy, filling every onlooking face - the only thankful blessing in this profoundly upsetting scenario.

"Ludwig!" bellows Master Robert, standing statuesque, "Where are you boy?"

Ludwig immediately recognises his master's voice and bounds over, nudging Master Robert's legs, licking his fingers...tail wagging as Master Robert leans down to pat him vigorously, "I've missed you, boy! I've really missed you!"

25

Walk on Ludwig!

"It's so awful!" starts Hester, pouring everyone a cup of tea at the breakfast table, "Master Robert just sits on the patio, all day - silently...in his own world."

"Does he say anything?" asks Jim, passing the milk jug to Jane, "...anything at all?"

"Nothing," replies Hester, shaking her head and closing her eyes in pity. "When he does speak - usually when someone's trying to help or bring him something, he snaps - bites their head clean off!"

"Will he ever see again?" enquires Joanna, turning her tea a whiter shade of milky, imagining how hard it must be to face a life in darkness.

"I overheard her Ladyship saying there's no chance, although they're arranging for Master Robert to see a specialist in London."

"What has this war achieved..." remarks Jim, sitting back in his chair and sighing deeply, "...other than death and mutilation... and stalemate!?"

"Daddy..." begins Joanna as she gets up from the table to get ready for school.

"Yes, Pet?" replies Jim, munching the last bite of his toast, "What is it?"

"Can you help me with something after school?" Joanna asks - forever inventive and beginning to visualise her idea, "I have an idea that might help Master Robert!"

"Sure," replies Jim, collecting the dishes and taking them over to the sink for washing, "come to the stables, and I'll see what I can do. Now hurry up and get ready for school - we need to leave in five minutes."

Joanna, Jane and June are fortunate. Lady Buttontrop believes, *"You girls are the future. You are my suffragettes! How can women change their circumstances without an extended education?"* She makes sure Jim takes them to school, and she pays for any books and fees, on the understanding the girls will stay in education beyond the recently increased school-leaving age of 14. Hester and Jim of course agree, often commenting, *"Her Ladyship always wanted a girl...and now she has three!"*

Joanna, Jane and Jean make their way back from school. Although Jim takes them to school, he can't always pick them up, so they end up walking the hour's walk home, often across fields - when they're dry. When they reach Fortuna House estate, Joanna climbs the stile and runs to the stables, leaving Jane and Jean to wander home to begin their chores - kindly agreeing to do Joanna's as well.

Joanna can't wait to show Jim her idea. She'd been told off twice for doodling it in class - the second time made to stand in the corner for fifteen minutes!

"So, run that by me again," says Jim, scratching his head and trying to decipher Joanna's scribbles, "...and slowly this time!"

"It's a special harness, Daddy!" repeats Joanna, now breathing normally, after arriving out of breath, "Like on a horse...but instead of soft reins, we make a rigid *U-shaped* bar...and then we attach the harness to Ludwig, and the bar becomes the handle for Master Robert, so they can go in and out of the house and around the grounds - Ludwig becoming Master Robert's eyes!"

"But Ludwig's going to run off at first sight of a rabbit," remarks Jim, trying not to pour cold water over Joanna's idea, "...and take Master Robert with him!"

"I'll train Ludwig!" replies Joanna, enthusiastically, "We'll attach a *leading* reign to the front, and I can lead Ludwig until he gets the hang of it and Master Robert feels confident to walk alone."

"Well, I admire your initiative, Joanna!" comments Jim, rubbing his chin - always keen for an engineering challenge, "We've got nothing to lose. I've got just the thing we can adapt..."

A few hours later, Jim and Joanna have created something very similar to Joanna's sketch. Joanna runs back towards the house and calls for Ludwig, who comes bounding around the corner - he may be 70, but he still thinks he's a young pup!

With a couple of adjustments, the harness fits Ludwig perfectly - although initially, it must be said, Ludwig wasn't very keen on wearing such a thing.

"Have you got an old driving whip I can have?" asks Joanna, unclipping the soft reins and holding Ludwig by the rigid bar.

"You mustn't whip Ludwig!" replies Jim, concerned that Joanna may be taking the horse analogy one step too far!

"As a treat-dangler," replies Joanna, "like dangling the carrot in front of the donkey!"

"I like it!" enthuses Jim, disappearing to fetch an old whip, "Dogs love to be rewarded and what better way to train him?"

"Exactly, Daddy." replies Joanna, smiling at Jim, before saying in an authoritative voice, "*Walk on*, Ludwig!"

Ludwig walks on...then trots on...then canters on until he's dragging Joanna towards the house. "Woaa, boy! Woaa!" shouts Joanna, then whispering under her breath, "I need to get him to obey me first before I take him anywhere near Master Robert."

Joanna asks her mother for some dog treats and attaches a piece of dried tripe to the end of the whip, putting the rest in her pocket for rewards. Grabbing the bar with her left arm and the whip with the other, Joanna entices Ludwig to walk back to the stables. She shouts various commands; *stables, left, right, stop, sit, walk on, circle left, circle right* - Ludwig, salivating and straining at the dangled treat, is rewarded when he responds correctly and learning that *pulling* and *running* result in no treat and a severe reprimand!

"I'm impressed." applauds Jim, admiring Joanna's persistence and watching Ludwig lead Joanna around the stableyard, calmly and cleverly. "What a clever boy he is!"

"Now watch this, Daddy!" shouts Joanna as she closes her eyes, "I'm doing it blind!"

Joanna experiences Master Robert's darkness, albeit with a mental picture of the stableyard, walking slowly, trusting Ludwig for every step and gaining confidence with every completed exercise - confident enough to make her way back to the house. "Ludwig. *House. Walk on!*"

With a few more hours of practice after school the following day, Joanna feels ready to engage Master Robert and walks Ludwig over to the patio.

"Hello, Master Robert!" announces Joanna in advance, having been told not to *sneak up* on Master Robert. "Ludwig is wearing something he wants you to feel."

Master Robert doesn't reply until Ludwig licks his hand, "Ah Ludwig, good boy!" he says, patting Ludwig on the head - stroking his neck until he discovers the harness, repeatedly patting, touching cold metal, finding the handlebar.

"Ludwig wants to take you for a walk," adds Joanna, hoping that Master Robert will begin talking. "He has a special harness for you to hold and he wants to be your eyes!"

"How can a dog become my eyes, Joanna?" dismisses Master Robert, becoming agitated and pulling his hand away from Ludwig's harness, "It's the blind, leading the blind!"

"We've been practising." defends Joanna, determined not to be defeated, "He can walk me to the stables and back and around the lake. Please, give him a chance. I'll be there to lead him until you're confident to be alone."

Master Robert says nothing. Two minutes passed in awkward silence. Then he reaches down, slowly and grabs Ludwig's handle and again, saying nothing, pushes himself to a standing position "I'm putting my faith in you, Joanna. Let's go!"

Joanna attaches her reins to Ludwig's harness and says, "Ludwig *Lake. Walk on!*"

Joanna, Ludwig and Master Robert, walk slowly and silently around the lake - Joanna leading less and less, as Ludwig enjoy walking beside his master again.

"You must talk to him," advises Joanna, delighted her idea seems to be working, "give him the correct commands and praise Ludwig wants to help you - he wants to be your guide."

Master Robert is overcome with emotion, triggered by Joanna's determination and Ludwig's love and ability, "Thank you, Joanna You've brought light into my darkness, and for this, I will be eternally grateful!"

Lady Buttontrop and Hester are watching everything from the kitchen window - it's the first time Hester sees her Ladyship cry. With tears rolling down her cheeks, Lady Buttontrop turns to Hester and simply says, "Thank you, Hester, thank you fo

26

If music be the food of love, play on!

Joanna races home after school every day for a week - eager to walk with Master Robert...eager to train Ludwig well enough for Master Robert to walk without her. Hester informs Joanna that she's seen Lady and Lord Buttontrop sometimes taking the reins and guiding Ludwig and Master Robert around the lake, much to the delight of Master Robert. The mood has undoubtedly lightened at Fortuna House, and no one feels like they're treading on eggshells anymore.

"Hi, Master Robert!" shouts Joanna as she approaches, smiling at Ludwig's unerring enthusiasm and delight to see her - his tail wagging ferociously as if every encounter is their first, "Are you ready for another walk?"

"Hi, Joanna!" greets Master Robert, now dressed in regular clothes and wearing dark glasses instead of bandages - all adding to his readjustment into *Civvy Street*, replying, "You bet! In fact, I'd like you to take us beyond the lake and do a lap of the woods."

"Of course!" Joanna says, excitedly, grabbing the reigns and helping Master Robert from his chair, "It's such a beautiful day with the sun streaming through the..."

Joanna stops mid-sentence, annoyed with her insensitivity.

"Don't stop, Joanna." says Master Robert, shaking his head for reassurance, "Please, don't worry what you say - you must treat me the same...as if I can see. I rely on you and others around me to articulate the world - give words to the pictures...the pictures I imagine in my mind."

"I'm sorry," says Joanna, caught in that bizarre human behaviour of apologising, even when something isn't their fault, "I mean, of course, Master Robert. It's such a beautiful day with the sun streaming through the trees and dancing along the floor, as the leaves shimmer in the light summer breeze!"

"Much better, Joanna," Master Robert says, his tone thankful as he nods his approval, "Much better, indeed!"

They round the lake and detour through the woods - Joanna taking more care to avoid large sticks and fallen boughs - following a naturally-made path which snakes its way around trees and bramble bushes. There are occasional skeletal structures - sticks and branches, propped against twisted wooden backbones, once clad in long gone bracken and soft spruce, signs of past summer mud-larking and unparented camping.

"Can we just stop a while," asks Master Robert, standing still and raising his left index finger to his mouth to request silence, "and just listen!"

"Sure," replies Joanna, "whatever you want, Master Robert."

Master Robert moves his head left and right, turned up and outstretched as if straining to hear the minutest of sounds. Joanna listens too and begins to discover and appreciate the different array of sounds. Birds are chirping - warbling, tweeting, cooing. Squirrels are darting - hopping, skipping and jumping. Bumbling-bees are buzzing and humming - *do-si-do-ing* from one flower to the next. Leaves are rustling like hands searching in a brown paper bag - hopeful for the last morsel or sweet. Crickets are *batting* their back legs like maracas in a rumba. A distant woodpecker is tap-tap-tapping - resting, tap-tap-tapping - repeating. Ludwig is licking and preening - occasionally head shaking with jowls flapping and saliva slobbering!

"When you don't have your eyes..." begins Master Robert, "...your ears and your nose takeover. Try it, Joanna! Close your eyes and listen to nature's music, and smell the day - today's unique smell - different to yesterday's or tomorrow's!"

Joanna closes her eyes. It's true. The sounds are more vivid, and the smells are more distinctive - as if she can hear the clouds moving and smell honey on the bee's breath! "You're right, Master Robert!" declares Joanna, "We don't use all our senses enough...in a way, our eyes make us lazy lookers!"

They both smile and continue through the woods, inventing a new version of *I spy. I spy with my little ear...* and *I spy with my big nose...something beginning with...*

The following day, Joanna arrives as usual to take Master Robert and Ludwig for another walk. However, Master Robert is sitting alone - Ludwig lounging by the lake, harness unhooked and left at Master Robert's feet. Master Robert has several unopened letters, resting on the table in front of him - all addresses, seemingly written by the same feminine hand - all French-stamped and postmarked.

"What's wrong, Master Robert?" enquires Joanna, softly, sensing his sadness, "Are you not up for a walk today?"

"Not today," simply says Master Robert, head down - yesterday's smile left somewhere in the woods, "I don't feel like it."

"Is it the letters?" asks Joanna, unaware of her directness, "Is it because you can't read them?"

Master Robert, reluctant to discuss, but given Joanna's helpfulness and positivity, eventually tries to explain. "They're from a girl I met in France - an English nurse who looked after me when I fell off my horse, early in the war. She doesn't know about my loss of sight, and she's still out there, looking after people who've caught this terrible Spanish flu."

"Would you like me to read the letters to you?" offers Joanna, thinking this the problem.

"It's not that, Joanna." replies Master Robert, "Why would she want anything to do with me now? Now I can't see...now I'm useless and rely on a dog to take me places..."

"I think you're feeling sorry for yourself, Master Robert," says Joanna, not pulling any punches, "and my Dad always says: *there's nothing worse than people who feel sorry for themselves!*"

Master Robert says nothing. He buries his head in his hands - taken aback by Joanna's frankness, finally whispering, "But how can I write to tell her...and express my feelings?"

"I can write for you," suggests Joanna, feeling awkward at becoming a *love letter* writer!

"That's very kind," remarks Master Robert, "but I won't be able to say what I really feel."

"Why don't you write her a tune?" says Joanna, "Compose your feelings in music?"

"If I can't write with a pen, how can I write with a piano?" dismisses Master Robert, now turning his face to the heavens in desperation.

"Have you tried?" poses Joanna, "You play the piano so well, and you can hear the music - you don't need your eyes!"

"Perhaps you're right." finally concedes Master Robert, holding out his hand for Joanna, "Please, help me to the piano."

Joanna escorts Master Robert to the living room and helps him sit at the grand piano, directing his hand to the inlaid sapphire -

the sapphire denoting middle C and dead centre. Master Robert is a little rusty at first but soon begins to get the hang of it. Joanna leaves him to it, agreeing to return the next day.

After racing home from school, Joanna approaches the patio, but Master Robert is nowhere to be seen. Then Joanna hears the most beautiful sound coming from the living room - Master Robert has created a tune that *sways* like a dancing couple. Heartbeats are pulsing - the girl, twirling under the boy's arms, then coming back together in hold.

"It's beautiful, Master Robert," compliments Joanna, closing her eyes to let the music take her. "She'll love it!"

"Do you think so?" asks Master Robert as the last few notes fade away.

"Definitely!" replies Joanna, "What's her name?"

"Her name? Her name is Poppy," says Master Robert with a fond smile, "and the tune is called, *Poppy: remember me!*"

Joanna feels a strange sensation - her eyes roll back and begin twirling inside her head as if exploring her mind and entering a spiralling tunnel of flashing lights and multicolours...making her travel forwards in space...making her travel forwards in time.

Time travels...

She opens her eyes to find she's sitting at the piano in her living room, wearing her green satin dress - seed-dibbler, resting at her feet...red and green keys both on show!

She's back to the present.

27

And they call it *puppy love!*

"You're joking, Jenny!" exclaims Joanna, staring at the computer in her playroom, "Eight kittens...Tipsy's had eight kittens? I want one!"

"Yeah, eight kittens, Joanna!" replies Jenny, lifting her computer and walking from her dining room into the kitchen, directing the camera at eight *balls of fluff*. "We didn't even know Tipsy was pregnant and came down this morning to find her licking and feeding eight beautiful kittens!"

"O.M.G!" shouts Joanna, viewing the kittens for the first time, "They're adorable...ahh...look at the one with the white feet...and the one with white ears..."

"You mean, *Sneakers* and *Phones!*" replies Jenny, directing the camera back on herself and cuddling Sneakers and Phones close for Joanna to see, "I'll ask my Mum if you can have one."

"I'd love one," says Joanna, pressing *print screen* to capture the kittens, "especially, Sneakers...but my Dad's allergic to cats...so unfortunately, it's a non-starter!"

"Such a shame, Joanna," remarks Jenny, "we don't get to see each other before school starts, and you can't have one of my cats. I'm thinking something, or somebody is plotting against us!"

Joanna tries to tell Jenny of her time travels, but all Jenny does, is rub her chin sarcastically and twizzle her finger around her temple, shouting, *"Cuckoo! Cuckoo!"* Joanna wants Jenny to visit so that they can time travel together, but as Jenny predicted, her

Mum isn't happy with her travelling by train alone - and now, Jenny has kittens to look after - eight beautiful kittens!

"I'm going to ask if I can get a dog..." begins Joanna, envious of Jenny's bundles of pet heaven, "...we've got the space, and my Dad says he loves dogs!"

"Sounds like a cool plan, Joanna," agrees Jenny, kissing the heads of Sneakers and Phones, "...oooh...I'd better put the kittens back...Tipsy's looking for them. Listen...I'll call you later!"

"I'm so jealous, Jenny." replies Joanna, moving the cursor to end the call, "*Chatcha* later!"

"Can I get a dog?" asks Joanna, walking into the dining room to find Trish on the sewing machine...again...and Roger flicking through a catalogue of light switches...again! "I mean, can *we* get a dog?"

"You can't even look after Regina!" replies Roger, still flicking through the catalogue, his green reading glasses perched on the end of his nose like a mad professor, "So, how will you cope with a dog?"

"Daddy's right, Joanna." adds Trish, also continuing to sew - her red reading glasses also perched on the end of her nose, accept more like an old granny than a mad professor, "A dog is a big commitment and a massive responsibility."

"Please, please!" begs Joanna, clasping her hands together and using her best *puppy* eyes, "I'll look after it...feed it...wash it...walk it..."

"You said that about the two goldfish...Katie and Pink," adds Roger, peering at Joanna over his glasses, "...and look what happened to them!"

"That wasn't my fault," defends Joanna, crossing her arms. "That was the next-door cat, and it was *you* who suggested putting them in the small pond!"

"That's right, Darling!" Trish adds, removing her glasses and biting one of the arms, "You said they'd be safe and..."

"...I thought they'd be safe under the metal grid," says Roger, wishing he hadn't brought up the topic of fish. "How was I to know, a cat would be cunning enough to fish them out for dinner!?"

"A dog isn't fish!" says Joanna, "It'll be a proper addition...man's best friend!"

"Perhaps we could get a dog," says Trish, beginning to see the advantages, "we had a dog growing up and absolutely loved her to bits."

"And you had a dog, Daddy," points out Joanna, "Wurzel!"

"Wurzel!" exclaims Trish, coughing a laugh, "After the scarecrow?"

"No...The Wurzels!" reminisces Roger, breaking into song and a West Country accent, "...*now, I've got a brand-new combine harvester, and I'll give you the key!*"

"Please, can we get a dog?" pesters Joanna, "Please?"

Roger looks at Trish and begins some form of telepathic communication - eyebrows moving like Morse code, lips pouting and un-pouting...eventually nodding in unison.

"We can get a dog!" proclaims Roger as Joanna runs over and hugs him.

"We'll get a rescue dog!" adds Trish as Joanna runs over and hugs her.

"Thank you, thank you!" shouts Joanna, "...and I know what we'll call it."

"And what's that?" enquires Roger.

"Ludwig!" announces Joanna, confidently, "Like Ludwig van Beethoven!"

"I like it!" replies Roger.

"So, do I!" agrees Trish, "So that's settled. We'll go and pick out a puppy at the weekend."

"Now go and get ready for Herr Mozhoven," instructs Roger, peering into his catalogue again - thumbing page after page to find his place, "he'll be here any minute!"

"Hello, Herr Mozhoven," greets Joanna, opening the door - dressed in her navy blue lace party dress, orange tights and silver pumps, reminiscent of her first lesson, "I'm getting a dog!"

"Dogs see the world in shades of yellow, blue und grey und hear twice as well as humans," announces Herr Mozhoven, breezing past into the living room, "...but why they're so obsessed with sniffing other dogs' bottoms, I'll never understand!"

"I'm calling it, Ludwig!" announces Joanna, following directly behind Herr Mozhoven.

"Ludwig!" simply says Herr Mozhoven, suddenly stopping in his tracks and pausing. "Ludwig?"

"Yes, Ludwig," repeats Joanna, "...after Ludwig van Beethoven!"

"Yes, I know who Ludwig is!" replies Herr Mozhoven, turning and staring into Joanna's eyes, "Have you played the green und red piano keys together?"

"No…no, I haven't," fibs Joanna, shocked by the intensity of Herr Mozhoven's stare and crossing her fingers behind her back, "I promise!"

"Sehr gut!" replies Herr Mozhoven, turning and reaching the piano - erecting his brass seat and diverting Joanna's attention back to her dog, "Ludwig. What ein great name!"

Joanna runs through her warm-up exercises and plays *Women: we salute you* and *Poppy: remember me*.

"Sehr gut!" says Herr Mozhoven, flicking his fringe and straightening his cravat, "Turn to page fifteen. You are ready for another tune."

"*Children: always grow up,*" reads Joanna, securing the pages, "What's this one about?"

"This is an early-Victorian tune around 1840," begins Herr Mozhoven, "when children worked in mills und factories from as young as five - doing all the boring jobs. Jobs adults were too big to do. Factory owners loved children because they were cheap und they could replace them easily if anything happened to them, which very often did - lost fingers und occasional loss of life!"

"Even girls?" enquires Joanna, shaking her head in disbelief.

"Even girls." replies Herr Mozhoven, nodding his head, "It annoyed factory owners when children grew up, which they have ein habit of doing…because they had to pay more money!"

The tune is repetitive like the monotony of a weaving machine. Interspersed with fluttering as if representing the machine, stopping to be cleaned or have its bobbins changed, then repeating, ending with what Joanna can only describe as the sound of a bird flying - being set free.

"Sehr gut, Yoanna!" ends Herr Mozhoven, returning his dismantled chair to his jacket breast pocket, "Good luck choosing Ludwig tomorrow. I will see you on Monday."

Joanna is baffled by Herr Mozhoven knowing she's getting Ludwig this weekend but immediately dismisses it - excited at the thought of having a dog and hearing the front door close. "I must tell Master Robert about *my* Ludwig!"

Sitting on the stool, Joanna lifts the seed-dibbler into position and without further thought, plays both keys at the same time.

Just as before, the red key makes the bassist, lowest, deepest, heaviest note and the green key makes the treble-ist, highest, shrillest, tightest note. Then fireworks, thunder and lightning and manic piano playing! Joanna closes her eyes for the crescendo - *BOOM* - blowing her away from the piano...making her travel backwards across the living room floor...making her travel back in time.

Time travels...

Joanna opens her eyes. She's not on a train or in Fortuna House or the old lodge - she's trapped in a massive loom, a woman shouting directions at her, a gruff man bellowing at her to hurry...the loom is about to start again!

28

It's a hard-knock life!

"Right a bit, Joanna!" instructs Peggy, the loom operator - taking advantage of this time to mop her brow and breathe deeply for renewed energy, "…and quickly, before Mr Miggins turns it back on!"

"I've nearly got it," replies Joanna, dripping in sweat - reaching as far as she can with her fingertips and straining to get enough purchase on the bobbin, accidentally and innocently dropped during bobbin-doffing, "…there, I've got it!"

Joanna passes the bobbin through the thread wall to Peggy's outstretched clammy hand and moves to a safe place inside the loom - adjusting her bonnet, just as Mr Miggins cranks up the machine to commence weaving once more.

The factory room is a regiment of machines. Duplicating tasks and teams, imprisoned and airless with windows kept shut to avoid fluff-stirring, making it unbearably hot…air conditioning and health and safety are still figments of the future!

Joanna isn't supposed to be in the loom while it's working, but someone must remove the fluff, so machinery doesn't become clogged or fabric contaminated, and someone must tie any broken threads - best done by small and nimble fingers - children's fingers - and girls' fingers better than boys' fingers.

If the loom must stop for any reason, it isn't making money, and if it isn't making money, someone must pay. That someone being Peggy, Joanna and even Mr Miggins, the foreman. *"Time is money!"* he incessantly says.

The dawning of industrialisation is double-edged - goods become more plentiful and affordable, but workers are heavily exploited...so the rich get richer, and the poor get poorer. Joanna can't understand why *goods* are called *goods* rather than *bads*, given the conditions she and her colleagues must endure! There are no unions to fight for common decency, protect the vulnerable or safeguard children. Stolen childhoods are woven into the fabric of society. There's no fun, no play, no time to discover and learn. Children are forced to grow up, too soon to become another cog in the hand-oiled machine, rather than allowed ambition and aspiration. Poverty and social position are rewarded with disease and malnutrition - the value of life at an all-time low - commercial slavery on a frightening and inexcusable level.

Peggy has the demeanour of a sixty-year-old - bent, bored and broken. She's only nineteen - still, a child herself, still wanting a family of her own, but faced with life as a loom *mule-spinner*...a *white donkey* working six days a week, from five o'clock in the morning until nine o'clock in the evening.

Joanna is a scaled-down version of Peggy - working the same hours and enduring the same conditions - groomed to replace Peggy or someone just like her. Neither Peggy nor Joanna is unique - the machine room is full of replicas. Factories, up and down the country practise the same processes and procedures - women and girls exploited for their dexterity and focus, men and boys, exploited for their physical strength. All are working like machines...for the machines...to feed the mouth of progress.

"Joanna, get yourself out of there!" orders Mr Miggins, checking his fob watch and worksheet, "Swap with Martha and start fetching buckets of water to dowse the floors!"

"Right away, Sir!" replies Joanna - her voice drowned by the drone of the machines, *slick-slacking* like old typewriter keys on an industrial scale.

Joanna fetches a bucket of water from the vast vat outside. She likes this job because she gets to breathe fresh air for a few minutes and splash herself with cold water. There is a temptation to drink the water, but everyone knows it's a gamble - this water has been collected from the local river without filtration or sanitation and comes pre-mixed with animal and sometimes human excrement. No one has put two and two together yet, but too many people are struck down with fever after drinking dirty water - Joanna will wait until suppertime when the water is at least away from the factory floor.

Moving up and down each machine aisle, Joanna uses a large wooden ladle, to spoon the water from her bucket and throws it to the floor. The bucket becomes lighter after every aisle and Joanna goes from struggling and water-spilling with two hands to almost skipping, single-handedly, back to the vat!

Although it's virtually impossible to talk to anyone on her rounds and never openly - only whispered snitches away from Mr Miggins eyes, Joanna catches up with her friends...the girls she shares a dorm with - the girls she calls *family* - her mother and father unknown, leaving Joanna outside the workhouse at birth too young to remember. Some girls get to go home with their mothers every night, but not many. Mr Dobbden, the mill owner prefers his workers on site - on call and totally devoted.

The other good thing about leaving her loom is the chance to see different stages of the textile-making process. Joanna is fascinated by the yards of fabric, rolled and stored like chocolate eclairs in a bakery. Some of the colours are vibrant and unbelievably beautiful, others are patterned or flower-covered like sweet summer meadows. Joanna pictures herself wearing a floor-sweeping dress with taffeta bow and billowing arms, delicately embroidered and laced...her hair, braided and bowed...her hands in buttoned and monogrammed elbow-length gloves.

Mr Miggins office is on the factory floor. He has a huge bin, full of discarded paper - covered in orders and numbers on one side, but blank on the other. Joanna helps herself to handfuls every time she can - when Mr Miggins isn't looking, of course, and puts them in her apron pocket. One time, she's fortunate! Mr Dobbden gives Mr Miggins a new pen as a small gift for his length of service and commitment to duty. Mr Miggins tosses his old *dip pen* and a one-third-full pot of ink into the waste bin, which Joanna immediately rescues - it beats a blunt pencil...especially one so small, Joanna can hardly hold! It means that, together with easy access to thread, Joanna can create her own sketchbook, albeit a sketchbook that reads as a factory order book when viewed backwards.

There's also an area in the factory where the fabric is checked for quality and consistency, and small lengths are often discarded - deemed unfit for further use. Joanna loves these - she collects them...again in her apron pocket and has a growing collection, which she hides in a special place in her dorm, under a loose floorboard by her bed. Every Sunday - her only day off, she sketches ideas for clothing and uses these offcuts to create *masterpieces*...helped by her close friend, Martha.

"There 'as to be somethin' better than a knee-length dress and white-aproned pinafore for workin' in the looms!" observes Joanna, dipping her pen in the black ink and beginning to sketch, "Somethin' fit for purpose and fun!"

"I'm fed up 'avin' to wear the same thin' every day!" agrees Martha, looking at the fabric offcuts laid on Joanna's bed, "Except Sunday, today, when we get to wear somethin' pretty!"

"I'm thinkin' somethin' with ventilation!" begins Joanna, scribbling an open-underarm, open-backed top with rear-opened sleeves, above and below the elbows. "...and padded knees and elbows and a buttoned front flap, startin' at the waist and movin' up the sides and over the front in one continuous arch," she says as she sketches, ink-dipping her pen continuously, to keep the line weight consistent, "and large pockets down each side...and an attached bonnet you can choose to wear up or down..."

Joanna begins to drape fabric over Martha like she's a tailor's mannequin, tacking and pinning as she goes. It's not long before it resembles her sketch, but it'll take another Sunday to finish - working after a full day in the mill is an impossibility!

29

Pride before a fall!

The following Sunday, Joanna and Martha finish the new work dress quite quickly - they manage to match patterned offcuts on the front, flowered offcuts on the back and double-stitch the pockets and the front flap for extra-durability.

"Turn around, Martha," says Joanna, wanting to view her handiwork, "It's great! How does it feel?"

"I love it!" enthuses Martha, flapping her arms like a frantic chicken, then air boxing an imaginary foe, "It's so lightweight and liberatin'. You've gotta 'ave one too!"

"Definitely!" replies Joanna as if the thought hasn't passed her mind, "It'll be much quicker, now we've made one…especially as we're the same size."

Martha removes her new work dress, and Joanna starts on the next, choosing striped offcuts for the front and plain colours for the back. She was right - they manage to complete the second work dress by bedtime. Now they both have a new work dress to wear in the morning.

"What are you two wearin'?" bellows Mr Miggins, looking over his worksheet, unsure whether to punish or praise. "I'll deal with you later. Get to your machines and start oilin'…we have fifteen minutes before the looms start weavin'!"

Joanna knows the room temperature rises over the day, made worse by a sunny day, but already she feels cooler and more able to carry out her tasks in the cramped conditions - crawling inside the loom and dripping oil into the machine joints, like a pianist tuning his piano!

"Oi, Joanna, you gotta make me one of those outfits!" shouts Peggy, pulling her clothes back and forwards from her body like a makeshift fan, "Anything'll be better than these 'eavy clothes!"

"Sure thin', Peggy!" replies Joanna, proud of her creation - happy to be the topic of factory gossip...initial mockers fast-becoming new clients as the day wears on and the smell of continuously worn workwear begins to waft like a boy's stinky sock drawer. "Maybe nex' Sunday!"

"I think we should petition Mr Miggins for you to make us all new outfits," adds Peggy, becoming conscious of her body odour, then laughing, "he might even want one!"

"Enough talkin'!" bellows Mr Miggins, "Get on with your work! I don't want to hear another dickie bird!"

Six hours later, around eleven o'clock, Mr Miggins comes over, bellowing, "Joanna, Martha! Get yourselves over here, right this minute!"

Joanna carefully exits the loom, thinking it must be change over time, then worrying she and Martha are in trouble for their new work clothes. Martha and Joanna, stand silently together in front of Mr Miggins - hands crossed behind their backs, preparing themselves for an ear bashing.

"One of the men is sick today, and I can't spare anyone else," begins Mr Miggins - Joanna and Martha, noticeably relaxing their shoulders in relief. "I need you to take a roll of the latest fabric design over to the shop. Mrs Miggins has Lady Stotton after some new fabric for her daughter, and she's not happy with the current selection. Do you think you can manage that...without droppin' it?"

"Sure, Mr Miggins," reply Joanna and Martha, looking at each other like it's Christmas! "We can manage!"

Joanna takes the front, and Martha takes the back, and they begin carrying the six-foot roll out of the factory and across the yard - avoiding men pushing trolleys and horses pulling carts. Neither has been to the shop before - neither allowed, hidden from view, and the shop positioned outside the factory walls. People travel from miles around to buy the unique fabric - *Dobby Fabric*, nicknamed after Mr Dobbden and special because its diagonal weave drapes like a soft waterfall.

Mrs Miggins is waiting by the shop door. Joanna can't believe how similar she looks to Mr Miggins - perhaps it's her permanently scowled fat face!

"Hurry up, girls!" bellows Mrs Miggins, "We can't keep Lady Stotton waiting."

Joanna takes the first step into the shop with no problem, but Martha trips on a cobble and shunts Joanna forwards - making her miss her footing, trip and fall flat on her face, at the feet of Lady Stotton. Martha is still standing - mouth wide open and expecting a massive telling off!

"You stupid children!" scolds Mrs Miggins, trying to squeeze past Martha, but failing.

"That's enough, Mrs Miggins!" says Lady Staunton, sternly, "Are you alright, child? Here, let me help you up."

Lady Stotton, dressed in the most beautiful dress Joanna and Martha have ever seen, and wearing the frilliest and fancy hat they've ever laid eyes on, picks Joanna up by her arm.

"Sorry, Ma'am!" says Joanna, "We're really sorry. 'Twas an accident. Promise!"

"Of course, child." calms Lady Stotton, turning to Mrs Miggins, "This is the job for a strong man, not two young girls. I suggest *you* take the roll, Mrs Miggins, and relieve these sweet innocent girls!"

Mrs Miggins takes the roll and places it on the counter, giving Joanna and Martha daggers - a look they know will mean serious trouble later!

"What's this?" asks Lady Stotton, picking up Joanna's sketchbook - accidentally dropped out of her front flap when she fell, "...and what are these fantastic outfits you're wearing?"

"That's my sketchbook," replies Joanna, sheepishly - looking at the floor...still expecting a telling off, "...and these clothes are new work dresses I've created...to make workin' in the weavin' room much cooler!"

Lady Stotton flicks through the sketchbook and walks slowly around Joanna and Martha, occasionally pulling at detail or grabbing a shoulder to move them right and left. Lady Stotton knows she must nurture this raw talent - remove Joanna from the clutches of oppression...offer her opportunities beyond *the run of the mill* before her light goes out forever!

"Mrs Miggins," Lady Stotton says at last, "I want to speak to Mr Dobbden, immediately!"

"Right you are, Lady Stotton," replies Mrs Miggins, disappearing through the back of the shop, "please, wait a moment, and I'll fetch him."

Mr Dobbden arrives. He's much bigger up close...and greasy.

"Good morning, Lady Stotton!" greets Mr Dobbden, bowing and shaking her hand, "How can I be of assistance?"

"This girl here..." begins Lady Stotton, turning and pointing at Joanna, "...what's your name, child?"

"Joanna," replies Joanna, unsure where this is leading.

"This girl here - Joanna." continues Lady Stotton, "She's coming home with me."

"I beg your pardon," stumbles Mr Dobbden, thinking he mishears.

"This girl here - Joanna!" repeats Lady Stotton, "Is coming home with me!"

"With all due respect, Lady Stotton," replies Mr Dobbden, becoming agitated, but maintaining a smile, "this girl belongs to me. She works for me, and I feed and clothe her!"

"Not anymore, Mr Dobbden!" replies Lady Stotton, "Name your price and add it to my bill!"

Mr Dobbden - flabbergasted, but seeing an opportunity to make money, begins mental arithmetic, staring at the ceiling and pulling the most bizarre faces!

"Excuse me, Ma'am," softly says Joanna, touching Lady Stotton's arm to get her attention. "What about Martha?"

Lady Stotton realises her oversight and turns to Mr Dobbden, "Joanna and Martha are both coming home with me. Otherwise,

I will be asking my husband to look into your affairs and treatment of child labour. Rumours are rife about your working practices."

Mr Dobbden realises this could get bad - Sir Stotton is a leading London barrister. He hurriedly dismisses Lady Stotton with a flick of his hand, "Take them. Take them both! No charge!"

"I will, Mr Dobbden, thank you!" says Lady Stotton simply, "…and Mrs Miggins, I will take the roll of fabric the girls brought over. Please, charge it to my account."

Joanna and Martha are dumbfounded and follow Lady Stotton out of the shop. Lady Stotton beckons her carriage and turns to Joanna and Martha. "Do you have any belongings we need to fetch?"

"No, Ma'am!" reply Joanna and Martha, "Just the clothes we're wearin'!"

"Very good." announces Lady Stotton, "Let's get you home to Fortuna House…I can't wait for you to meet my daughter, Bibby!"

The footman assists Lady Stotton into the horse-drawn carriage, then offers his hand to help Joanna and Martha into the carriage like they're two princesses.

Joanna and Martha have been set free!

But Joanna can't help but shed a tear for Peggy - where's *her* Lady Stotton?

30

Not just a pretty face and a dirty neck!

"Thank you, Elsa," says Lady Stotton, leading Joanna and Martha through the front door of Fortuna House and into an impressive hallway - there are large staircases either side...two large doors straight-ahead and corridors leading left and right. "Please, prepare the top-front room for Joanna and Martha. They will be staying with us."

"Very good, Ma'am," replies Elsa, searching for Joanna and Martha's bags, but soon realising they don't have any.

"On second thought, take Joanna and Martha upstairs and run them a bath," instructs Lady Stotton, looking again at Joanna and Martha's filthy faces. "I'll rummage through Bibby's old clothes and bring something fresh for them to wear!"

"Very good, Ma'am," replies Elsa, smiling at Joanna and Martha. "Follow me, girls. Let's see how clean you scrub up!"

Joanna and Martha stand in amazement, watching Elsa turn two tap things at the end of a metal bath - hot water magically streaming out and filling the room with steam. Bath night at the mill was only once a week and a rapid affair - shared with many others and always in dirty, cold water and rarely with soap!

"Here's a bar of soap and a towel each," says Elsa, delighting in Joanna and Martha's happy faces, "I suggest you get in together and help each other clean the parts you can't reach...here's a loofah...that may help, and give your hair a very good wash. I'll come back in fifteen minutes to see how you're getting on."

"Please, don't throw our clothes away!" asks Joanna, handing her new work dress to Elsa, "They may not look like much, but they mean a lot to us!"

"Of course, Miss Joanna," replies Elsa, turning to go upstairs and prepare their room, "I'll lay them on your beds!"

Martha and Joanna look at each other - still not computing what's happening - then bursting into fits of giggles.

"Miss Joanna!" says Joanna, in a swanky voice, "Elsa called me *Miss!*"

Joanna and Martha scramble around - splishing and splashing, occasionally spilling, watching their grime disappear like grease-covered dishes dipped in a magic cleaning solution. The resulting tidemark resembles an oil-slicked shoreline, the water a darker shade of brown. Martha and Joanna are puffed up with a healthy tint of reddened skin and wrinkled prunes for fingers and toes!

"My word," says Elsa, returning with toothpaste and toothbrushes, "I don't recognise you both! Miss Joanna, you have the most beautiful brown eyes and hair and Miss Martha, the deepest scarlet red hair I've ever seen...and eyes like the greenest emeralds only found in deep South African mines!"

Joanna and Martha wrap a towel around their bony bodies, smelling the fresh fragrance and feeling the soft pile against their cheeks - if they died now, they'd die happy!

"Here's a toothbrush," announces Elsa, handing Joanna and Martha black bone-handled toothbrushes with swine bristles, "and some toothpaste powder!"

Dental hygiene is a low priority at the mill. Joanna and Martha are lucky - their milk teeth are not too long gone, and their adult teeth are still salvageable. They think back to the endless screams of other children in the dorm suffering toothache - rotten teeth falling out or hand-pulled with pliers. Joanna and Martha feel the tingling sensation of deep cleansing fresh mint - they can't help but smile and not just any smile, a smile to end all smiles. Joanna's teeth, a crowded *crossbite* with a slight *underbite*, Martha's teeth, pretty good considering - just a crooked right canine!

"Now brush your hair," instructs Elsa, handing them a hairbrush - observing Joanna, scratching the living daylights out of the back of her head and Martha, using both hands to rub her head like a crazy person, "...and I'll check for head lice. We can't have you infesting the house - it's a nightmare!"

Unfortunately, Joanna and Martha's hair is tangled and knotted, made worse by burrowing and nesting nits. Having their knots untangled is the most painful thing either of them has had to sit through - and coming from a mill, that's saying something!

"How long, Elsa?" complains Joanna, tears rolling down her cheeks, "Please, stop!"

"It's for your own good," replies Elsa, not liking the torment she's putting the girls through, but knowing she can't take them downstairs until it's done, "I promise, we'll never let it get this bad again!"

"You promise?" pleads Martha, used to unkept promises, "You're not just sayin' it?"

"I promise." says Elsa, trying hard to be gentle, "Nearly there!"

Once this difficult job is out of the way, Elsa gets Joanna and Martha to put each foot on her knee so she can cut their toenails - overlong and curling like talons, then fingernails...*snip, snip, pinging* as clippings fly off and hit the inside of the bath!

"Make sure you dry in between your toes." says Elsa, placing a towel on her lap and again beckoning Joanna and Martha to place each foot on her lap, "I'll do it this time, but you need to do it by yourself in future, so you don't get *foot fungus*. See, you have a little, but it's not too bad - I think we've caught it just in time."

After Joanna and Martha have helped Elsa pick up the nail clippings and wiped the bath and floor, they follow her to the top level.

"This is your room," announces Elsa, leading them into the left room, overlooking the front of the house, "You can decide which beds you want, but I've put your work dress here, Miss Joanna," Elsa points to the far-right bed, "...and your work dress here, Miss Martha, in the closest bed. Just make your way downstairs when you're ready - I'm off to help Cook prepare afternoon tea."

Beside each work dress, Lady Stotton has laid a beautiful dress and bonnet - blue-lace dress with matching bonnet next to Joanna's, white-embroidered dress with pink bonnet next to Martha's and a pair of black leather shoes at the foot of each bed - slightly worn, but as good as new in their eyes!

Next to their dresses is a knee-length, shorts-like garment with frills along the bottom hems. Neither Joanna nor Martha have seen such things, but presume they must be some sort of undergarment - knickers!

Joanna and Martha are like cats who got the cream with their beds - curved dark wood with soft feather-filled mattresses, looking more like the carriage they arrived in than the beds they're used to - wooden *coffin* boxes with straw-filled mattresses, laid directly on the floor in regimental lines!

"These beds are fit for a queen!" shrills Joanna, swallow-diving onto hers, "...and it's gonna be great to be off the floor!"

"Yeah," replies Martha, swallow-diving onto hers, "...no more mice scratchin' at your box as you're noddin' off!"

Joanna and Martha put on their dresses, "I think I prefer your pink bonnet," considers Joanna, "...and this blue one will match the fine blue flowers in your dress!"

"My shoes are too tight!" says Martha, agreeing to swap bonnets, but struggling with her shoes.

"My shoes are too long." replies Joanna, "Let's swap!"

"*These* shoes are too long!" says Martha, shaking her head in disbelief!

"And your shoes are too tight for me, too!" adds Joanna, looking for a better solution, "Why don't we wear one of each and share the pain?"

"Then swap each day," agrees Martha, "to share the pain even further!"

They giggle and make their way downstairs - nervous and unsure where to go...strangers in a strange house!

"Ah, there you are!" says Lady Stotton, spying Joanna and Martha from the rear drawing room, "Come through - there is someone I would like you to meet."

Joanna takes the lead and guides Martha into the drawing room, suddenly aware of the room's grandeur - floor to ceiling bookcases, oil-painted portraits, plush red velvet drapes, fine-upholstered green-flowered sofas and chairs and the grandest of grand pianos, centrally positioned in front of the bay window.

"Well, if I didn't know it was you," begins Lady Stotton, studying Joanna and Martha, "I would say you had been replaced by two smartly-dressed princesses with long flowing locks and the prettiest faces I have ever seen!"

"Thank you, Ma'am!" reply Joanna and Martha, bashfully, "We absolutely luved the 'ot bath and thank you so much for these luvly clothes."

"You are very welcome," replies Lady Stotton, glancing at their feet, "although it looks like a visit to the cobblers is needed!"

Joanna and Martha look at their feet and realise how odd they appear - one small foot and one long foot as if one foot's been shrunk in the wash!

"Girls, please, meet my daughter, Bibby," introduces Lady Stotton, giving an open-armed gesture to put Joanna and Martha at ease, "…and Bibby, please, meet Joanna and Martha…two fantastically talented girls, who need our love and support."

"Hello, Joanna. Hello, Martha," greets Bibby, shaking Joanna and Martha by the hand and curtsying - not fully, just right foot placed behind left, followed by a small knee bend, "it's a pleasure to meet you both. Mother has been telling me all about that dreadful Mr Dobbden and the mill - it sounds frightful!"

"It's a pleasure to meet you, too!" responds Joanna, trying to replicate the curtsy, but mixing up her feet, deciding to bow instead.

"It's a pleasure to meet you, too," adds Martha, copying Joanna, but mastering the curtsy!

"It's like we're going to be sisters!" adds Bibby, smiling with excitement, "I have always wanted sisters, and just as I am *coming out*, I finally get some!"

"I think what Bibby is trying to say," says Lady Stotton, walking over to the wall and pulling a strange lever - twice, "is that we want you to treat our home like your home and consider us as your family!"

"Thank you, Ma'am." replies Joanna, "You're both very kind...what's *coming out?*"

"*Coming out* is the start of finding a suitor," begins Lady Stotton - Bibby giggling behind a raised hand.

"What's a suitor?" asks Martha, confused by all these new terms.

"A *suitor* is a suitable match for marriage!" replies Lady Stotton, looking fondly at Bibby. "When a girl reaches an age of maturity - sixteen in Bibby's case - and is educated and skilled in piano playing, singing, painting, needlepoint, has memorised the monarchy, studied classical history and geography...then they are ready to be introduced into society and be married within a year or two!"

"Married!" replies Joanna, staring at Bibby, "That's so grown up!"

"You rang, Ma'am?" says Elsa, appearing at the door - bowing her head. Joanna and Martha, begin to realise what the strange lever is.

"Ah, Elsa," says Lady Stotton, smiling and pointing at the window, "it is such a lovely day, I think we will take afternoon tea on the patio!"

'Very good, Ma'am," replies Elsa, turning to leave.

'And, Elsa!" adds Lady Stotton, looking at Joanna and Martha, 'Joanna and Martha will be joining us for supper. Sir Stotton will be arriving back from London at around six o'clock, so please inform Cook, we will eat at six-thirty."

'Very good, Ma'am," replies Elsa, again bowing her head before disappearing.

Joanna and Martha have afternoon tea with Lady Stotton, then spend time with Bibby, walking around the lake and familiarising themselves with Fortuna House. At six-thirty, they sit at the long dining room table - Joanna and Martha on one side, Bibby opposite, Lady Stotton at one end and place setting for Sir Stotton at the other.

'Sorry, I'm late!" apologises Sir Stotton, bounding into the dining room - kissing Lady Stotton and Bibby on the foreheads and sitting head of the table, before finally noticing Joanna and Martha, "Well, who have we got here?"

'Take no notice of Sir Stotton," begins Lady Stotton, giving Sir Stotton a stern look, "his bark is worse than his bite!"

'Yes, please, forgive me." replies Sir Stotton, softening with a deep breath, "Pleased to meet you, girls!"

'This is Joanna and Martha," adds Lady Stotton, smiling at the girls, "I rescued them from that diabolical Mr Dobbden…at the mill."

'Dobbden, you say," nods Sir Stotton, pouring himself a glass of wine. "Despicable man, a man born with no compassion

"Joanna is a brilliant drawer, and budding fashion creator and Martha is her faithful assistant." informs Lady Stotton, promoting the girls, "I will show you her sketchbook when we retire to the drawing room."

"Very good." replies Sir Stotton, nodding his head and giving Lady Stotton his full cooperation, "I will look forward to it...now let's eat - I'm starving!"

"Mushroom soup!" announces Elsa, entering the room after Lady Stotton rings her small table bell, "Followed by asparagus in breadcrumbs, venison pie with fresh potatoes and carrots and finishing with Cook's new sweet - rhubarb pie!"

Joanna and Martha are used to a bowl of broth, a piece of bread and a lump of cheese. They've never seen a mushroom, let alone taste one - asparagus sounds like *a pair of shoes,* but they're hoping that's not the case. Venison pie sounds like a pie made by *Venison,* the famous chef and son of *Veni* and rhubarb sounds more like something Mr Miggins might say; *"That's bar-rhu-barb!"*

"You work your way from the outside in," says Bibby, helpfully, seeing Joanna and Martha staring at the array of cutlery, set either side of their soup bowl, "just follow my lead and you can't go wrong!"

After what can only be described as a veritable feast and the tastiest food Joanna and Martha have ever eaten, they all retire to the drawing room - candle-lit by wall sconces and a central chandelier.

"This is very good, Joanna!" praises Sir Stotton, passing her sketchbook back to Lady Stotton, "I can certainly see you are wasted at the mill."

"Joanna and Martha helped bring some fabric over for Bibby's *coming out* dress," adds lady Stotton, passing the sketchbook back to Joanna, "which is how it all started. They fell and spilt everything at my feet!"

"Talking of Bibby's *coming out*," enthuses Sir Stotton, "I've created a little tune to celebrate this momentous occasion."

"Sir Stotton is an accomplished pianist!" informs Lady Stotton, smiling admirably at him, "He trained at the Viennese School of Music, before passing his bar exams."

"It's a beautiful piano," remarks Joanna, not wanting to appear stupid by not knowing what *bar exams* are, "I've only seen our church piano, which is nowhere near as grand!"

"This, Joanna and Martha, is a *Bösendorfer 90!*" brags Sir Stotton, demonstrating its unique feature, "Built with two extra keys, accessed by these levers, to commemorate Beethoven's death and presented to my music teacher - the man who taught Beethoven!"

Joanna and Martha nod politely, but have never heard of Beethoven - they only know the inside of a mill...how to change bobbins, oil looms and tie broken threads.

"Old *Mozy*, my music teacher, passed away recently," adds Sir Stotton, "and I bought it...paid too much for it, mind you, but it is one of a kind, and so was *Mozy!*"

"I can't wait to hear the tune, Father," encourages Bibby - she's heard the piano story too many times to count.

"Yes, of course, Bibby!" responds Sir Stotton, giving her his full attention, "Right, it goes something like this..." Sir Stotton plays the tune, adding commentary to the changing tempo, "The tune is repetitive..." he begins, turning his head to look at everyone, "...like the routine of everyday life!" he adds, shrugging his shoulders and giving a wry smile, "...but then it's interspersed with *fluttering*..." he says, again looking around - his fingers rippling up and down the keys, "...to represent milestones - the important things you remember and cherish!" he adds, turning to give Bibby and Lady Stotton a loving glance, "...then it repeats..." he says, swaying his head and torso side to side, "...and then it ends like a soaring bird..." he concludes, running his right hand in an upward scale, repeating, getting softer each time, "...as my beautiful daughter leaves home...to start a new life!"

"I love it, Father!" compliments Bibby, walking over to the piano and giving Sir Stotton a hug from behind, "What is it called?"

"I haven't given it a name yet!" says Sir Stotton, staring at the ceiling, as if the tune's name is written there. "But if I had to give it a name, it would probably be...*Children: always grow up!*"

Joanna feels a strange sensation - her eyes roll back and begin twirling inside her head as if exploring her mind and entering a spiralling tunnel of flashing lights and multicolours...making her travel forwards in space...making her travel forwards in time...

Time travels...

She opens her eyes to find she's sitting at the piano in her living room, wearing her navy blue lace party dress, orange tights and silver pumps - seed-dibbler, resting at her feet...red and green keys both on show...

She's back to the present.

32

Eeny, meeny, miny, moe!

"Joanna, darling!" calls Roger, repeatedly knocking on the bathroom door, "You've been in the shower for twenty minutes now. Please, finish up and get ready - we want to get to the dog rescue centre by ten, so we don't waste the day...do you hear me, Joanna...JOANNA?"

"YES, WHAT IS IT DADDY?" shouts Joanna, finally hearing, moving her head out from beneath the shower.

"OH, NEVERMIND!" shouts Roger, exasperated, "JUST, HURRY UP!"

Trish had rung the centre the day before to make an appointment - Saturday mornings are very popular!

"This is exciting." remarks Trish, looking back at Joanna in the back seat and smiling, "Our first dog!"

"I can't wait!" replies Joanna, cuddling Snonkey and making her body go rigid in excitement, "I couldn't sleep, thinking about it!"

"Me neither," adds Roger, tapping the postcode into the satnav and pressing *go*, "that's why I'm looking *ruff* this morning!"

"*Barking* mad, more like!" jokes Trish, throwing another pun.

"I think we should *paws* the jokes!" jests Joanna, hearing the groans from the front seats.

"A friend of mine had a dog with no nose!" remarks Roger, looking at Joanna through the rear-view mirror.

"How did he smell?" responds Joanna, already knowing the punchline, but playing along.

"Awful!" delivers Roger, laughing at his own joke - something he does more and more these days!

Roger, Trish and Joanna meet *Becky* at the reception, who takes them to the kennels and lets them wander freely from pen to pen like visitors in an art gallery, moving from one painting to the next.

"Hey, that one looks like Grandpa Jo!" says Roger, pointing at a boxer - bored and with bloodshot eyes.

"They say dogs look like their owners." remarks Trish, ignoring Roger's slight at her father, pointing at a long-nosed collie, "Perhaps this one's for you, Roger!"

"I think a Brad Pitbull Terrier is more fitting!" jests Roger, hoping the next dog will fit the bill but doesn't!

"It's so hard to choose," says Joanna, ignoring her parent's jokes, seeing each dog as a Victorian mill worker, "they all look so sad! I wish we could take them all home!"

"I know, Sweetheart!" responds Trish, hugging Joanna's neck, "It's hard to believe some people mistreat or abandon animals."

They walk past a few more kennels, almost to the end, when Joanna suddenly stops and calls out, "Ludwig! I've found Ludwig!"

At the back of pen sixteen is a border-collie, poodle mix - a black mongrel with a white stripe running up its nose, into a long fringe and down two floppy ears, just like Beethoven's wild and eccentric haircut!

"I see you've found *Beetroot!*" says Becky, arriving to give more details, "He's a lovely dog with a beautiful temperament. His previous owner sadly passed away recently, and there is no one to take him. If you look at him in direct sunlight, he has a purple tinge - we're guessing that's why he's called Beetroot!"

"I want to call him Ludwig!" remarks Joanna, "Do you think I can?"

"If he were a puppy, I'd say yes," replies Becky, grimacing slightly, "but given he's nearly five, I think it would be too confusing for him!"

"Think of him as *Ludwig van Beetroot!*" says Roger, trying to put a positive spin on it.

"I like it, Daddy!" says Joanna, staring into Beetroot's eyes, "Full name, Ludwig van Beetroot...*Beetroot* for short!"

Joanna chooses a red collar and a green lead and proudly marches Beetroot out of the kennels to the car. As she fastens her seatbelt, Beetroot places his head on her lap, as if they've known each other for years.

"Look, Mummy!" shouts Joanna, cuddling and massaging Beetroot's ears, "He's lying on me!"

"It's his way of saying, thank you." replies Trish, "You've made each other very happy. Well done, Joanna!"

Quiet and contented, Joanna daydreams as they drive home - thinking about Lady Stotton, Martha and Bibby...how much she wants to see them again...see how her life would unfold if she were still there...

"Can you teach me how to sew?" says Joanna, out of nowhere, "...and how to use the sewing machine?"

"What brought this on?" replies Trish, reminding herself how the brain of a ten-year-old works. "Of course, I'd be delighted to...it's a very handy life skill!"

"Can you teach me, too?" adds Roger, "Surely a fat-fingered bloke like me can get the hang of it."

"Of course, you can." says Trish, "The more, the merrier, then we can spread the load!"

"I've had an idea I want to make." continues Joanna, "It's called *Joannamals* - handbags in the shape of animals!"

"I like it!" replies Roger, thinking of his preferred animal, "Can you make me a green snake bag for all my rulers?"

"Sure, Daddy," replies Joanna, "...but first I thought I'd make *Snonkey* - a white, donkey-shaped bag and *Blippo* - a blue, hippo-shaped bag and *Beetroot* - a purple, dog-shaped bag, especially for Herr Mozhoven!"

"What a clever idea!" compliments Trish, turning around and giving Joanna the thumbs up, "I can show you how to put in a simple zip as well...to make them really good."

"Brilliant!" replies Joanna, patting Beetroot - now licking Joanna's arms and hands.

"Please, don't let the dog lick you!" says Roger, shaking his head and pulling a face of disgust, "Dogs lick everything and everywhere - its unhygienic!"

"I love it, Daddy!" replies Joanna, rotating her hands for *a full-lick* experience.

"I used to love it when I was younger," adds Trish, "...and I'm still here. If she wants to...let her!"

"As long as you wash your hands when you get home and before you eat anything," concedes Roger, shuddering at the thought.

"Of course, Daddy," agrees Joanna, "I don't know why you don't like it...it's fantastic!"

Monday afternoon arrives. Joanna waits at the front door - dressed in her red party dress, hair in two green bow-tied bunches, Beetroot sitting at her feet and in her hands...the purple dog-shaped bag she's made for Herr Mozhoven.

"Good afternoon, Herr Mozhoven!" greets Joanna, opening the door at five o'clock on the dot, "Did you have a good weekend?"

"Ya! Thank you, Yoanna." replies Herr Mozhoven, "Und I see you have Ludwig!"

"His name's Beetroot!" informs Joanna as Beetroot sniffs Herr Mozhoven as if Herr Mozhoven's trying to smuggle something into Fortuna House, "His full name is: Ludwig van Beetroot!"

"Sehr gut!" says Herr Mozhoven, automatically, as if he didn't hear the play on Beethoven's name, continuing into the living room and preparing for the lesson.

"I made this for you, Herr Mozhoven," says Joanna, holding out her Beetroot *Joannamal*, "Your very own *Beetroot* - somewhere for you to keep your chair and tuning equipment!"

"Thank you, very much," replies Herr Mozhoven, taking the bag and bowing, "This is very thoughtful. I very much appreciate it. Now let's proceed with the lesson!"

Joanna runs through her warm-up exercises - plays *Women: we salute you*, *Poppy: remember me*, and *Children: always grow up*.

"Sehr gut!" says Herr Mozhoven, flicking his fringe and scratching the end of his nose, "You are progressing very well. When do you go back to school?"

"Next Monday." replies Joanna, butterflies fluttering inside her stomach at the thought, "It will be my first day at my new school!"

"I see," says Herr Mozhoven, closing his eyes for a moment and breathing in, as if smelling something. "Turn to page eighteen. There is another tune I would like you to learn."

"*Fashion: faux pas or formality!*" reads Joanna, securing the pages, "What's this one about?"

"This is ein tune written in 1765...some say by Mozart when he was your age, but it's unproven...about fashion during the mid-eighteenth century." begins Herr Mozhoven - knowing Joanna's interest in fashion and trying to think of a simple way to describe it, "When pale skin with red blusher is the *thing* und men und women wear enormous wigs und women wear huge hooped dresses - impractical und impossible to sit in!" continues Herr Mozhoven, tittering, as if remembering some incident, "Then comes *industrialisation* und mass production - the lower classes emulate higher classes for the first time...affordable coloured-cotton looks as good as expensive satins und silks!" continues Herr Mozhoven, gripping his jacket lapels with both hands and feeling the cloth with his thumbs. He concludes, "*Enlightenment* results in a backlash against extravagance, in favour of comfort und leads to revolution und dissent, und the birth of democracy for the common people - the platform for the way the world works today!"

"Wow!" exclaims Joanna, astounded by Herr Mozhoven's description, "All that from fashion!"

Dogs are big scaredy-cats!

"This tune is more difficult, Yoanna," explains Herr Mozhoven using his telescopic baton to point at the notes, "You have to reach over und play ein high chord every third bar und reach over und play ein low chord every fourth bar like this!"

Herr Mozhoven, as usual, makes the tune look easy, reaching far right every third bar and far left every fourth bar. Joanna can't believe how completely different this tune sounds, compared with the others, as if it needs to be played with more hands and has real energy - something vibrant and exciting...almost childlike!

"Now you try!" encourages Herr Mozhoven, reminding Joanna of **E**very **F**ancy **G**irl **A**lways **B**oils **C**racking **D**evilled **E**ggs **F**irst and **G**ood **A**ustrian **B**ourgeois **C**hefs **D**o **E**at **F**ine **G**oulash **A**lso, "...from the top!"

Joanna tries her best, playing each note in turn like a toddler taking its first steps, until it begins to flow - as if she knows instinctively, which notes come next and anticipates its natural progression...made more fun with far-reaching left and right three-note chords.

"Sehr gut!" praises Herr Mozhoven, preparing to depart, "Please practise this. After you go back to school, I will be teaching you once ein week, so let's make the most of this week."

"Only once a week!" disappoints Joanna, frowning, "That's a shame. I'm enjoying learning!"

"You don't stop learning if you practise every day!" reassures Herr Mozhoven, aware that practice is the most difficult part of learning. "I will fix the piano levers," continues Herr Mozhoven oblivious to Joanna's look of surprise, "...it is not right for ein piano of this grandeur to remain broken."

Joanna and Beetroot follow Herr Mozhoven to the door and bid him farewell - Joanna smiling...seeing Herr Mozhoven walk down the drive with a big purple *dog*, dangling from his shoulder!

"O.M.G!" shrills Joanna, running back into the living room and talking to Beetroot like he's another human being, "Herr Mozhoven's going to fix the piano! It will stop me playing both high and low notes, together! It will stop me travelling back in time!"

Joanna fetches the seed-dibbler from beneath the sofa, talking continuously to Beetroot, "If this is my last chance, then I'm taking you with me, Beetroot. You can be the first dog to time travel!"

Sitting on the stool, Joanna calls Beetroot onto her lap, lifts the seed-dibbler into position and without further thought, plays both keys at the same time...

Just as before, the red key makes the bassist, lowest, deepest, heaviest note and the green key makes the treble-ist, highest, shrillest, tightest note. Then fireworks, thunder and lightning and manic piano playing! Joanna closes her eyes for the crescendo - BOOM - blowing her away from the piano...making her travel backwards across the living room floor...making her travel back in time! Unfortunately, Joanna can't stop Beetroot *freaking out* during the thunder and lightning - unable to hold both him and the seed-dibbler simultaneously...watching him jump down and run out of the room like a big scaredy-cat!

Time travels...

Joanna opens her eyes. She's not on a train or in the old lodge or *trapped* in a massive loom. She's sitting at a harpsichord - the piano predecessor...in front of the bay window in Fortuna House!

"Sit up straight, Yoanna?" orders the governess, looking at Joanna down her nose - not in a snobbish way…it's just the way she looks

"Sorry, Meine Dame!" replies Joanna, addressing her in a formal German manner - the governess, a Viennese Austrian, "I think need a bigger pillow to sit on…this one's too soft, and it's making me slouch."

There is tittering behind Joanna!

Joanna turns around to see a similarly aged boy, sitting upright and stiff in another chair like hers - a regular dining chair improvised for harpsichord playing. He's well-dressed - in a green satin long waistcoat and knee-length breeches, white shirt with yellow cravat, white stockings and silver-buckled black slip-on shoes, hair, swept-back and bow-tied into a small ponytail.

"That's enough, Willie!" scolds the governess, fetching an extra pillow and gesturing for Joanna to stand, "It will be your turn soon und I am expecting good things!"

It immediately silences Willie.

Joanna looks down at her sea blue satin floor-length dress billowing out from the waist - silver-buckled black slip-on shoes poking out beneath. She feels a thin white hat on her head and swept-back brown hair, sticking out like an Alice headband.

"Now sit, Yoanna." orders the governess, taking her position to the side of the harpsichord, "Und try again…from the top!"

Joanna plays the harpsichord - an instrument sounding more like a high-pitched plucked violin than a piano and not as big as a piano, but just as elegant. She's much happier with the large pillow, raising her closer to the keys.

"Sehr gut, Yoanna." comments the governess, after thirty minutes, "Now swap with Willie!"

Joanna leaves the music book and slides off the chair, taking her

"Right, Willie," begins the governess - Joanna, now sitting on Willie's chair, "turn back the page und start from the top! Let's see if you can do better than Yoanna!"

"Yes, Mutter," replies Willie, realising his informality too late, "...I mean, Meine Dame!"

Joanna thinks it's funny that Willie is the governess's son - allowed to stay at Fortuna House and study with Joanna, in return for reduced tuition fees. Joanna's parents - Henry and Liza Bucket with new-found wealth from revolutionising the simple water pail, want Joanna to get a good education so she can fit into higher society...something Henry and Liza are trying hard to achieve, but finding difficult due to their humble backgrounds.

"No, Willie!" scolds the governess, "It is obvious you have not been practising enough, unlike Yoanna!"

Joanna sees the governess give her a smile and nod of recognition - which doesn't happen often. Not because Joanna isn't deserving, but the governess has very high standards!

Joanna watches the governess teach Willie as if he's a stranger - her forehead wrinkling with every wrong note and un-wrinkling with every right note. Her immaculate floor-length dark grey satin dress, matching her pulled-tight auburn hair, held in a perfect bun...a bun, any baker would be proud!

Suddenly, the drawing room door swings open and in march Henry and Liza - Henry, clutching an opened letter.

"Sorry, Governess," interrupts Liza, smiling from ear to ear - her face, flushed either with excitement or red make-up, applied on top of her whitened-face, "Mr Bucket has some fantastic news!"

"It would appear Herr Mozart and his son, Wolfgang, have accepted our invitation to come to Fortuna House and perform a recital," relays Henry, half-reading, half-summarising the letter, "as an extension to their European Tour!"

"Who are Herr Mozart and his son, *Wolfman?*" enquires Joanna, unsure what all the fuss is all about!

"Wolf...*gang*...Mozart," corrects Henry, continuing, "is a child prodigy - an amazing composer and musician from Austria...lauded around royal circuits...throughout Europe!"

"But why is he coming here?" puzzles Joanna, still confused.

"Your father was lucky to hear the Mozart family perform in London recently..." adds Liza, bubbling over with excitement, but not wanting to steal Henry's thunder.

"...and when I was talking to Herr Mozart after the concert," continues Henry, smiling at Liza for allowing him this indulgence, "and mentioned that I have a daughter the same age as Wolfgang and a governess and music teacher from Vienna, in Austria - also with a ten-year-old son, his ears pricked up, thinking it could be a much-deserved break for Wolfgang, to come and interact with children his age...away from the prying eyes of London!"

"I have heard of the Mozart family," contributes the governess, formal and to the point, "Leopold und Anna Marie und their children - daughter, Maria Anna und son, Wolfgang Amadeus ...both brilliant musicians! It is sehr gut!"

"That's right, Governess." responds Henry, pleased to have her endorsement, "The letter says mother and daughter will remain in London, but the father, Leopold and son, Wolfgang, will be coming!"

"Coming tomorrow!" shrills Liza, "Tomorrow at midday. We have no time to prepare!"

"Please, don't become too concerned, dear Liza," calms Henry, "They're not royalty - just two normal people like us...albeit one with an amazing talent!"

34

Dressed to impress!

The following morning is bedlam. Everyone gets up at the crack of dawn and is given tasks to complete - by eleven o'clock...to give one hour to change into their *best clothes!*

Joanna and Willie are charged with assisting the governess in preparing the drawing room for the recital. Henry has a shopping list to buy as many things as he can from the local town - often, items must be ordered, so you only get what is available on the day.

"Why don't you take Joanna and Willie with you?" suggests Liza, informed by the governess, Joanna and Willie are becoming bored and beginning to play up.

"I'd rather not, dear Liza." replies Henry, strongly shaking his head, "They'll just slow me down, and I don't have time for shenanigans!"

"Very well, dear Henry." responds Liza, knowing Henry's probably right, "Hurry back!"

Henry walks quickly to the newly erected stables and takes the single horse-drawn two-seater carriage - it's faster and easier to park.

"Joanna! Willie!" shouts Liza, looking to relieve the governess, "Perhaps you would like to go and pick some flowers from the meadow - brighten up the place and add some pleasant fragrances!"

While Joanna and Willie run off to pick flowers, Liza helps the maid prepare the guest bedrooms and instructs the cook what to prepare for lunch, afternoon tea, evening meal and breakfast -

...err Mozart and Wolfgang, scheduled to leave at ten o'clock the following morning. Liza isn't used to having servants - she finds it difficult to give orders and can't help assisting whenever she can.

Henry arrives back. Liza and the maid help unload the groceries - it's all hands on deck.

It is the first time, Henry and Liza have had visitors - especially such distinguished visitors as Herr Mozart and son, Wolfgang - since finishing renovations and extending Fortuna House from modest manor house into magnificent mansion...and they want everything to be perfect!

Walls are panelled to dado height, then papered in the most expensive Oriental paper money can buy - the hallways are in the classical geometric style, and the drawing room resembles wooded scenery with chirping birds and freshly flowering blossom. Sofas, chairs and tables, are hand-crafted by Thomas Chippendale, in the trendy *Rococo style*. French porcelain ceramics adorn equally beautiful and decorative sideboards and cabinets. Wooden floors are covered in the most intricate and detailed, hand-woven, Persian rugs. Ceilings and cornices are finely plastered like carefully embroidered hems. There are gilt-framed mirrors - some large and ornate, some narrow and straightforward, positioned to reflect light and add illusions of depth. Fireplaces are grand and ornate - architectural in scale and proportion.

There is also a life-size portrait painting of Henry, Liza and Joanna hanging at one end of the drawing room - painted by leading artist of the day, Joshua Reynolds...founding father of the Royal Academy!

The rear garden is landscaped by *England's greatest gardener* - Capability Brown, creating a multi-tiered and stretched vista with infant woods planted either side, a central circular lake with sprouting water-features, formal topiary and groomed beds, laid close to the house. Marble statues are perfectly positioned for maximum effect.

Henry and Liza certainly have an eye for detail and excellent fashion sense.

Everything goes to schedule, and everyone begins changing into best clothes at eleven o'clock. Joanna and Willie are ready first - wearing pretty much the same as yesterday...watching out for their visitors from the first-floor window.

"They're here!" shout Joanna and Willie - seeing the four-horse-drawn carriage pull into the driveway...running downstairs to stand by the front door.

Liza sweeps downstairs in her first-time worn, and huge hooped bulbous satin rose dress. The sleeves, expanding at the wrist to reveal ruby red satin lining and matching left and right gold bracelets, her hair pleated and plaited with an interwoven decorative headpiece.

Henry is already waiting, suited and booted - wearing a long flowing curly grey wig, a long navy blue satin waistcoat and jacket, both with gold-embroidered edging and buttons, matching navy blue breeches, white stockings and silver-buckled black slip-on shoes.

"We certainly scrub up well!" jokes Henry, opening the door and stepping out to welcome Herr Mozart and Wolfgang, "We look a million guineas!"

The footman assists Herr Mozart and Wolfgang from the carriage and passes two suitcases and a wooden stool with an elegant handle at the bottom - which when turned, adjusts the stool height. Henry directs the footman to the stables, to rest and feed the horses in preparation for the return journey.

"Welcome, Leopold and Wolfgang," greets Henry, shaking each by the hand and helping with the luggage, "I trust your trip was uneventful...no highwaymen!"

"There was ein incident one hour out of London with ein broken spoke, but other than that...nothing!" replies Herr Mozart, following Henry through the front door, encouraging Wolfgang to hurry - obviously tired from the two-day trip and dragging his feet.

"Herr Mozart," begins Henry, gesturing towards Liza, "may I introduce Madam Bucket..."

"How do you do." greets Liza, invisibly curtsying beneath her gigantic gown and offering her hand, as if to show off her rings. "Welcome to our humble abode!"

"Enchanted, Madam Bucket!" replies Herr Mozart, cupping Liza's hand - bowing and kissing the top of her hand, "It is ein pleasure to make your acquaintance."

"...and this, Herr Mozart," continues Henry, gesturing to Joanna, Willie and the governess, "is my daughter, Joanna, our Austrian governess and her son, Willie."

"Delighted to make your acquaintance, Sir!" greet Joanna, Willie and the governess, each curtsying or bowing.

"The pleasure is all mine," replies Herr Mozart, bowing to each in turn. "Now let me introduce my son, Wolfgang!"

Wolfgang moves from one person to the next, avoiding eye contact and bowing half-heartedly, adding, "No, really, the pleasure is all mine!"

Henry escorts Herr Mozart and Wolfgang to the guest rooms, to freshen up, agreeing to reconvene in thirty minutes for lunch outside on the back lawn.

Herr Mozart comes out to the back garden, dressed almost identically to Henry, but dark green instead of navy blue. Wolfgang is following...dressed in a long scarlet-red silk jacket and matching breeches, a long silk waistcoat in a grass green colour, white shirt with yellow cravat, yellow stockings with gold-buckled, sapphire blue silk slip-on shoes and a grey wig with a yellow bow-tied ponytail.

Joanna and Willie haven't seen anything so wonderful - they feel decidedly dull by comparison!

"Those yellow stockings are positively shocking!" Joanna whispers to Willie, acknowledging how only a child can get away with such fashion statements, "...and who wears blue shoes with red? I love it!"

Henry and Liza are perfect hosts, lavishing their guests with enough food to feed a small army.

"Why don't you take Wolfgang to see the woods," suggests Liza to Joanna and Willie, recognising social awkwardness between newly introduced ten-year-olds, "and maybe have a game of horseshoes...before the five o'clock recital."

It isn't long before shyness is replaced with fun and frivolity. Joanna, Willie and Wolfgang get on like a house on fire - sometimes forgetting they're wearing *best* clothes and that Wolfgang is dressed in his recital gear!

"Wolfgang!" shouts Herr Mozart - always expecting decorum and feeling slightly uncomfortable, seeing his son rolling around on the grass, "I think you should come und calm down...your recital is due to start in fifteen minutes!"

"Yes, that's a good idea." agree Henry and Liza, beckoning Joanna and Willie, "There will be plenty of time to play after supper!"

Everyone ventures into the drawing room for the recital, while the maid clears the garden.

"I can't wait to sit down, dear Henry." whispers Liza, having been on her feet all afternoon, "My feet are killing me in these shoes!"

"Fater!" announces Wolfgang, standing at the harpsichord and staring at the dining room chair, "I need my playing stool!"

Just as Herr Mozart turns to fetch it, Liza sits down - her huge hooped dress unforgiving...the large *dome* lifting upwards and outwards, revealing Liza's knickerbockers for all to see!

"Oh dear, dear Henry!" shrills Liza, blushing behind her made-up red cheeks, "This is the most impractical fashion ever created!"

"Oh dear, dear Liza!" replies Henry, noticeably blushing - stepping in front to hide her undergarments, but failing...helping Liza stand...after four attempts!

Joanna, Willie and Wolfgang are giggling - they think it's hilarious! The governess soon puts an end to their laughs with one of her *down the nose* looks.

Herr Mozart returns with Wolfgang's playing stool, and Henry returns with a three-legged milking stool for Liza.

Wolfgang makes himself comfortable at the harpsichord, placing never-to-be-viewed music sheets on the stand and eating chocolate from a secret bag in his coat pocket!

Henry tilts Liza's dress and inserts the stool - which is immediately *swallowed* from view! Liza sits down on the stool with an audible sigh - still looking ridiculous as her huge hooped dress concertinas...making her look like her legs have sunk eighteen-inches into the floor!

35

Great balls of chocolate!

Wolfgang begins to play. An immediate hush descends - everyone transfixed like an audience witnessing magic and not believing their eyes...although, in this case, not believing their ears!

Young Mozart plays note combinations never previously combined, describing *heaven* in minute detail - dreams appearing reality...making sense out of chaos!

Joanna sits and revels in Wolfgang's ability to make playing look sickeningly simple - so much so, she swears, she sees Wolfgang nod off at one point, actually playing blind...the music, created and engraved in his mind, guiding his fingers around both keyboards and playing masterpiece after masterpiece, for all to enjoy.

Herr Mozart sits, eyes closed, familiar with the music, but relishing every moment - proud of his little boy and his ability to do things that most accomplished adult musicians only aspire.

The governess is in seventh heaven, not having to sit through novice renditions from Joanna and Willie - the tables reversed as Wolfgang gives her a lesson in musical mastery...her eyes, water-filled and overcome with emotion and disbelief.

Henry and Liza are delighted to be entertaining such sought-after guests - playing on *their* harpsichord...in *their* drawing-room...in *their* home!

Even Willie sits silently, appreciating genius!

Joanna thinks it's funny that, as every tune ends, Wolfgang delves into his right pocket and secretly takes another chocolate, putting it in his mouth with a disguised scratch of his left cheek, and seeing him turn around and occasionally give, what can only be described as a chocolate smile - teeth, appearing knocked out like some old crone. She starts observing noticeable changes in

Wolfgang's demeanour, as he becomes restless and overactive...his playing becomes harder and faster!

Herr Mozart opens his eyes and becomes disturbed - clenching his lips and shaking his head...knowing what's about to happen...

Wolfgang suddenly stops playing harmonious music and begins playing hard five-fingered chords with both hands - running the back of his fingers up and down both keyboards...doing the unthinkable of adding words...standing up and kicking his stool backwards, as it glides, then tips and crashes to the floor with a huge bang! Wolfgang, then placing his right foot on the keyboard and bashing the high notes - changing to his left foot and bashing the low notes...screaming, "Goodness, gracious, great balls of chocolate!"

Joanna and Willie find themselves tapping along, rocking their torsos and rolling their heads - triggered by something beyond their control...they just *wanna get down* and dance!

"*WOLFGANG AMADEUS!*" screams Herr Mozart, erupting from his chair, "That is enough!"

Henry, Liza and the governess are speechless - they have never seen a child behave like this.

"Apologise, Wolfgang!" orders Herr Mozart, turning to Henry and Liza - ashamed of his son's outburst, "This is what happens when you eat too much chocolate...you have some sort of reaction! I thought I'd confiscated all your chocolate balls?"

"I'm sorry, everyone!" apologises Wolfgang, shrugging his shoulders and giving a final chocolate smile, "I don't know what comes over me...I get bored of playing the same old tunes und want to play something rebellious und non-conformist!"

"Wolfgang did this in front of ein roomful of politicians!" explains Herr Mozart, trying to make light of it, "Ein real faux pas or so I thought. They were jeering und cheering like monkeys in ein zoo!"

"Please, don't give it another thought." consoles Liza, placing her hand on Herr Mozart's shoulder, "It was truly a magical recital!"

"Yes! Superb!" agrees Henry, giving Herr Mozart, a *kids-will-be-kids* look, suggesting, "Perhaps now is a good time to take supper."

"Yes, that sounds like ein wonderful idea!" replies Herr Mozart, following Henry and Liza through to the dining room, everyone else following suit.

Supper unfolds without incident, other than Willie knocking over his water and creating a mini river - Herr Mozart diving for cover to avoid embarrassingly soaked breeches!

Joanna, Willie and Wolfgang are excused from the table while Henry, Liza, Herr Mozart and the governess remain to swap more stories - the governess and Herr Mozart working out if they have more mutual acquaintances in Vienna, already discovering they use the same butcher, baker and candlestick-maker!

"What would you like to do, Wolfgang?" asks Joanna, leading Wolfgang and Willie back into the drawing room, "Perhaps you could teach us a simple tune..."

"Of course." replies Wolfgang, happy to be with people his age, "Perhaps ein tune we can play together!"

"I love your playing stool!" remarks Willie, lifting it off the floor and placing it back at the harpsichord, "Beats an improvised dining chair!"

"Have it," offers Wolfgang, enjoying the shock in Willie's face, "I can get another when I return to London!"

"I couldn't possibly take this!" replies Willie, being polite, but desperately wanting it, "What will your father say?"

"He will not mind," responds Wolfgang, thinking of a tune for them to play, "He will see it as repayment for my bad behaviour."

"Thank you, Wolfgang," appreciates Willie, shaking Wolfgang's hand, "I will cherish it forever!"

"Think nothing of it." replies Wolfgang, wondering what all the fuss is about, "It is just ein playing stool!"

"Did you know, you both share the same initials!" points out Joanna, looking fondly at Willie and Wolfgang - slightly envious of Willie's gift, "W.A.M!"

"What is your full name, Willie?" asks Wolfgang, enjoying the coincidence, "I am Wolfgang Amadeus Mozart!"

"I am Wilhelm Albert Mozhoven!" replies Willie, also enjoying the coincidence of sharing something with their new-found friend.

"We should inscribe our initials in the underside of the stool!" suggests Wolfgang, reaching for a brass tuning tool in his pocket, "We can use this!"

Wolfgang and Willie turn the stool upside down and scratch *W.A.M*, adding the year *1765* to capture this moment in time. Not wanting to exclude Joanna, Wolfgang reaches into his music sheet leather case and pulls out a red leather-bound book, handing it to Joanna, adding, "Yoanna, I would like you to have this new book I'm reading."

"'The History of Little Goody Two-Shoes'," reads Joanna, looking gratefully at Wolfgang, "Thank you, so much. I look forward to reading it!"

"I think you will prefer it to me!" replies Wolfgang, smiling, "It is like the Cinderella story, but instead of ein glass slipper, it is about ein orphan with only one shoe...given two, by ein rich gentleman. It makes her very happy - she tells everyone...und this is as far as I have read!"

"What tune are you going to teach us?" asks Joanna, placing the book on the harpsichord - keen to play with the maestro, adding, "...but remember, we're nowhere near as good as you!"

"You stand on my right - my *treble*, Yoanna und play these three keys when I say," instructs Wolfgang, showing Joanna, then turning to Willie, "...und you stand on my left - my *bass*, Willie und play these three keys when I say."

Joanna and Willie practise their three keys, ready for Wolfgang's prompt.

Wolfgang begins playing - every third bar, looking at Joanna and every fourth bar, looking at Willie.

Joanna and Willie are beside themselves with joy as they complete their three-fingered chords without mistake - all *high fiving* when Wolfgang plays the last note!

"Encore!" shout Joanna and Willie, twisting Wolfgang's arm. "Encore! Encore!"

After playing the tune three more times, Joanna suggests they play the tune for the grown-ups - when they eventually come through, Willie and Wolfgang agreeing. "What shall we call it?" poses Joanna, hoping to name it first, "How about - *All for one and one for all?*"

"That is gut!" replies Wolfgang, nodding, "...but perhaps given my earlier outburst - *Fashion: faux pas or formality* is more apt!"

Joanna feels a strange sensation - her eyes roll back and begin twirling inside her head as if exploring her mind and entering a spiralling tunnel of flashing lights and multicolours...making her travel forwards in space...making her travel forwards in time!

Time travels...

She opens her eyes to find she's sitting at the piano in her living room, wearing her red party dress - seed-dibbler, nowhere to be seen...Herr Mozhoven at her feet...tools laid out, fixing the piano levers!

She's back to the present.

36

Back to school!

"What are you doing, Herr Mozhoven?" enquires Joanna, looking at his intricate brass tools, laid out meticulously in a red velvet pouch.

"As I said, Yoanna..." replies Herr Mozhoven, puzzled and irritated by her question, "...I am fixing the levers to open separately as intended!"

"Is it working?" asks Joanna, hoping the answer will be *no*, but suspecting *yes*.

"It is easier than I thought!" replies Herr Mozhoven, adjusting a few screws on the removed brass panel, "I should have done it ages ago...when I first came!"

Joanna realises her time travels are well and truly over - now committed to memory...only the music book a reminder. It fills her with both anger and regret - anger that she can't continue and regret that she didn't say goodbye or ask more questions!

"There you go." exclaims Herr Mozhoven, packing away his tools and standing up - trying each lever in turn with success, "As gut as new!"

Beetroot wanders into the living room and plonks himself in the bay window - Joanna, disappointed with his failure to partake in her time travels. Herr Mozhoven puts his tool pouch in his *Beetroot* and closes the zip. Joanna is delighted Herr Mozhoven is using her *Joannamal!*

"Now turn to page eighteen und play *Fashion: faux pas or formality!*" instructs Herr Mozhoven, sitting on his expanded brass seat, "From the top!"

Joanna goes through the motions, still upset by Herr Mozhoven's fixing of the levers.

"Everything OK, Yoanna?" enquires Herr Mozhoven, giving Joanna a concerned look, "You don't seem your bubbly self, today."

Joanna blames it on *feeling unwell* and nervousness at *starting a new school.*

"Let's leave it for today!" announces Herr Mozhoven, packing everything into *Beetroot.*

Joanna walks Herr Mozhoven to the door.

"Gut luck at your new school," encourages Herr Mozhoven, turning to give Joanna a huge smile, "I'll be thinking of you!"

"Herr Mozhoven..." begins Joanna, unsure whether to continue with her question, "...can I ask you something?"

"Of course, Yoanna!" replies Herr Mozhoven, retracing his steps, "What is it?"

"What's your first name?" asks Joanna, expecting Herr Mozhoven to decline an answer - watching him hesitate before finally replying.

"My first name..." begins Herr Mozhoven, leaning closer to Joanna - realising Joanna has played both extra piano keys and travelled back in time, "...is Wilhelm!"

"...and do you have a second name?" further asks Joanna, staring back at Herr Mozhoven - unsurprised by his reply and seeking further confirmation.

"Ya, I do, Yoanna! ...it's Albert!" replies Herr Mozhoven, giving, what Joanna is sure is a wink, before reaching into his inside jacket pocket and pulling out a green leather-bound book, tied shut with a red ribbon, continuing, "Now I have fixed the piano...und both keys cannot be played together," adds Herr Mozhoven, giving Joanna a knowing look and a wry smile, "I would like you to have this picture book."

"Thank you, Herr Mozhoven," responds Joanna, accepting the book - her eyes widening and mouth opening, as she unties the red ribbon and opens the book to find an eclectic mix of drawings, paintings and black and white photographs...stuck inside like mementoes in a scrapbook, "What are..."

Joanna's voice peters out - she is speechless as she flicks through each page, ogling at every picture. Willie and Wolfgang - Herr Mozart - Henry and Liza Bucket - the governess - Martha - Sir Stotton, Lady Stotton and Bibby - Elsa - Mr Dobbden - Mr and Mrs Miggins - Peggy - Master Robert - Ludwig - Lord and Lady Buttontrop - Emmeline and Millicent - Jim and Hester - Jane and Jean - Mr Moss-Hogan... William - Lady Fitzroy...*Fitzy* - Charlie and Harrie - Mary, Mollie and Maud - June and Judy - David, Derek and Dillon - Dandelion, Daisy, Petunia, Primrose, Foxglove, Hollyhock - Jenny - the *Bösendorfer 90* - Fortuna House!

"This is our secret, Yoanna!" smiles Herr Mozhoven as he turns and walks away, bidding farewell with a circular waving of his right hand, adding, "Think of this book as a leaving present!"

Joanna smiles, cuddling Beetroot and watching Herr Mozhoven disappear - one moment there, the next moment, gone...vanishing into thin air like a deleted computer image. She shakes her head continuously and whispers, "Bye, Mozy. I'll never forget you!"

Joanna knows she will never see Herr Mozhoven again and hugs the picture book - the book that will enable her to continue travelling back in time and revisit all the wonderful characters she's met...whenever she feels like it!

There are empty pages, ready to insert new experiences. Joanna sees this as a sign - she is meant to come to Fortuna House and play her part in its history. It gives her strength to face the future with excitement - even look forward to starting a new school!

Joanna spends the rest of the weekend catching up with Jenny on the computer and completing her latest instalment of *Joanna Jaws*. Roger gives her a haircut - at least that's what he calls it! It's more a case of perching Joanna on a high stool, placing a makeshift gown around her torso, brushing her hair to a gathered length on her back, cutting three inches off the bottom - as straight as he can make it and give further attention to sticking out loose strands, when Joanna's hair is brushed back into its usual style!

"Why can't I go to the hairdressers?" complains Joanna, staring at her *boring* haircut in the mirror. "All my friends do!"

"When you're older." responds Roger, tucking his *salon scissors* into their plastic pouch, "When it makes sense to have a style other than long straight hair!"

Sunday evening involves a hot bath, clipped toe and fingernails and quick *nit check* - just in case, Trish, commenting, "I don't want to be the Mum to receive a call, informing me my child has triggered the next school infestation!"

"Sleep tight." says Trish, kissing Joana on the cheek - about to switch off Joanna's light, "Sweet dreams!"

"Mummy!" says Joanna, sounding like a question!

"Yes, dear?" replies Trish, waiting for the inevitable question, "What is it?"

"Can Beetroot sleep on my bed?" asks Joanna, knowing she's pushing her luck, justifying, "Just tonight...the night before I start my new school!"

"Nice try, Joanna." replies Trish, giggling at Joanna's persistence, "Dogs don't rationalise like humans. He doesn't know it's your first day at school and he's perfectly happy in front of the stove...warm as toast! Night, night!"

The following morning is bedlam - Roger and Joanna both starting new chapters...Roger's first day at his new job and Joanna's first day at her new school.

"There you go." says Trish, plonking boiled egg and soldiers in front of them, "This'll give you energy for your big days!"

"Thanks, Mummy," says Joanna, straw-sucking milky tea, taking a soldier and dipping - sending the yolk up and over like an erupting volcano...taking care not to spill anything on her new uniform, "I love *dippy eggs!*"

"Yes, thanks, Mummy," says Roger, pulling Trish's leg, feeling ten years old again, also sending yolk up and over - sipping tea...taking care not to spill anything on his freshly washed and ironed white shirt. "You're the best!"

Trish sits in the driving seat - Roger in the passenger seat, Joanna in her normal back seat position, Beetroot beside her...Snonkey and Snonkey-Joannamal on her lap!

"Are you nervous, Roger?" asks Trish, giving him a reassuring smile, "You'll be fine...just try to keep your jokes to a minimum!"

"Will do!" replies Roger, leaning over and kissing Trish, as she drops him off first, "See you tonight." turning to Joanna to give words of encouragement, "And good luck to you, Joanna. I want to hear all about your first day when I get home...and remember

Joanna...*Girl Power!*" says Roger, sounding cringingly hip and making it worse with his clenched fist, finishing, "You'll warm to the *stinky boys*...I promise...your mother did!"

Trish drops Joanna outside the school gate, thinking it best Joanna goes in on her own - blowing her a kiss and shouting, "Pick you up at three-fifteen. Good luck, Darling! I'll be sending you good vibes...and remember, never look back...only forwards!"

Joanna ventures into the playground - not recognising anyone...nearly gets knocked over by two boys playing *it*...and ducking to avoid a miss-kicked football!

"Are you, OK?" enquires Joanna, finding a girl with scarlet red hair and the greenest eyes she's ever seen - sniffling as she rubs the back of her right foot...shoe, discarded on the floor.

"I hate new shoes," replies the girl, looking at Joanna and mustering a smile, "I always get blisters...even if my mother gets them *big enough to grow into!*"

"Do you want a plaster?" asks Joanna, searching her Snonkey-Joannamal, "I packed some for this very problem!"

"That's very kind!" replies the girl, taking the plaster and applying it to her weeping wound, "What's your name?"

"Joanna!" replies Joanna, closing Snonkey's zip and putting it back around her shoulder, "What's yours?"

"Martha," replies Martha, replacing her shoe. "I love your bag!"

"I made it!" Joanna replies proudly, "They're called *Joannamals* and this one's called Snonkey - as in snow-white donkey...I can make you one if you want!"

"Absolutely!" Martha responds, excitedly, wiping her face - tears well and truly gone, as the pain subsides, "How cool is that?!"

"What's your favourite animal?" asks Joanna.

"A pig!" replies Martha, snorting and puffing out her cheeks!

"And your favourite colour?" further asks Joanna.

"Blue!" states Martha, staring at the sky - watching geese, flying overhead.

"A blue pig!" announces Joanna, "I'll make you, your very own *Blig!*"

"Thanks a lot, Joanna!" appreciates Martha, looking at her watch, "What form are you in?"

"6M!" responds Joanna, hoping that's right.

"Me, too!" announces Martha, "Me, too!"

The bell rings. Martha takes Joanna to 6M.

"Morning, children!" greets Miss Mossan, sitting - red pen poised to tick the green-covered register, "Can I see who's here and who isn't?"

Joanna looks around at her classmates - predominantly girls, interspersed with the odd stinky boy!

"Before we start formal lessons," begins Miss Mossan, closing the register and beaming at the children, "I thought it would be nice if we went around the room and found out what everyone got up to during the holidays! Who's first?"

There's a show of hands - some extremely eager, trying to point as high as humanly possible.

"We have a new girl..." informs Miss Mossan, rechecking her register, "...Joanna Pulton!"

Joanna looks up, not having put her hand up, not wanting to be first!

"Yes, Miss." responds Joanna, digging deep and thinking of *Joanna Jaws*, "I'm over here!"

"What did you get up to during the summer?" asks Miss Mossan, gesturing for Joanna to stand.

"I got a new piano…" begins Joanna, before the teacher interrupts to admonish another girl.

"Sarah Goode!" sternly shouts Miss Mossan, wagging her finger - Joanna mishearing…thinking she says *sehr gut!* Before Miss Mossan repeats, "Sarah Goode! Sit down, pay attention and listen!"

Joanna waits patiently for Miss Mossan to finish with Sarah Goode.

"Right, Joanna! Sorry about that! Now…where were we…" restarts Miss Mossan, smiling at Joanna, "Right children, let's hear all about Joanna and the piano…!"

Joanna takes a deep breath and launches into it, "Hi, my name's Joanna, and I'm ten years old…"

THANK YOU FOR READING

I HOPE YOU ENJOYED AS MUCH AS I ENJOYED WRITING

JOANNA AND THE PIANO

GAVIN THOMSON

BOOKS BY GAVIN THOMSON

JOANNA AND THE PIANO

ISAAC AND NEWTON'S APPLES

TWINNING TALES SHORT STORIES

MMXVIII

I

31755589R00110

Printed in Poland
by Amazon Fulfillment
Poland Sp. z o.o., Wrocław